A Box of Sand

Richard Rapp

A BOX OF SAND

This is a work of fiction. All of the characters, names, incidents, organizations, and dialogue in this novel are either the products of the author's imagination or are used fictitiously.

iUniverse books may be ordered through booksellers or by contacting:

iUniverse
1663 Liberty Drive
Bloomington, IN 47403
www.iuniverse.com
1-800-Authors (1-800-288-4677)

ISBN: 978-1-4917-5565-5 (sc)
ISBN: 978-1-4917-5564-8 (e)

Library of Congress Control Number: 2014921876

Print information available on the last page.

iUniverse rev. date: 02/11/2015

chapter 1

My Story

THE CAR SEEMED TO SENSE where I wanted it to go. It navigated every twist and turn on the Inter-Boro Parkway as if there was a magnetized track it was riding upon. I had always been certain that this parkway was unsafe for driving. It had to have been designed and built by a madman who wanted to stop drivers from Brooklyn getting to Queens or the reverse; drivers getting from Queens to Brooklyn. I was certain that was the reason they never published the figures of the amount of accidents on this particular parkway.

When I turned off the Inter-Boro, the car made two lefts almost without my turning the wheel at all. It stopped at the gate of the cemetery apparently a split second before I applied the brake. When the gate swung open it took the right turn directly toward the office. It slowed and came to a stop once again as if it was driven by an unknown mystic driver.

I rolled down the window. The sun blazed into my eyes.

"Where are you going?"

The woman had appeared as if when the gate swung open, she was catapulted out of her office to a place that landed her by the driver's side window. Her heft partially blocked the sun from my eyes. I could barely see a worn face that had forgotten how to smile.

I handed the woman the slip of paper that had the grave site marked on it.

"That's new, isn't it?"

"Three days ago."

"You know where it is?"

"Yes, I do."

"You mind waiting here just a sec?"

She hobbled away before I could answer. I minded, but what the hell, everyone has rules. The sun bathed the car again until she returned holding a thick dog-eared book. She thumbed through some pages.

"Brandeis, right? Three days ago, yes, that's right."

"Right."

"You want a Rabbi?"

"No."

"You're sure? They can help."

"I'm sure; no Rabbi."

"They can make it easier for mourners especially if this is your first visit. First visit after the burial, I mean."

No change in her look.

"No Rabbi, thanks."

I gunned the motor.

"You should leave some rocks; Brandeis will know you were here."

She turned and went back toward the office; she turned twice in my direction, shook her head and disappeared behind the door to the office.

The woman's appearance destroyed whatever directional principle my car had been operating under. I got lost twice and had to find and then ask a grave-digger where my grandfather's grave was. He looked at the paper I handed him and then told me, "Back up, then straight and two rights and a left as soon as you can and you're there buddy. Need one of them Rabbis? They know where everyone is who called it quits."

He didn't even crack a smile.

"No thanks. Back up, two rights and then a left. Thanks."

I took back my piece of paper and backed up out of the aisle my car was in. Straight ahead, two rights and a left; my car's directional system had been fully restored.

I stopped in front of a mound of freshly piled dirt that had a slat of white lumber stuck into it with the name "B-R-A-N-D-E-I-S" printed from top to bottom in black block letters. I got out of the car.

There was a grave stone close to the mound of dirt:

"E-V-A B-R-A-N-D-E-I-S", it read. My grandmother died roughly three years before. Memories of her flashed across my brain. I saw her with her false teeth, always a lousy fit, moving in her mouth as if they were swimming. She adjusted them with her tongue, never her fingers.

"Who needs to know?" she would say. "I know, *'genug iz genug'* ."

I smiled at the memory. She 'cheated' when we played casino and when she was caught, she always blamed it on her glasses.

"They don't see, either," she said in Yiddish.

Memories.

I thought a solo visit to my grandfather's grave without any other family members present to intrude on my thoughts, would ease some of the pain of his dying. It didn't work the way I had hoped it would. I stood in front of the pile of dirt with the marker on it. There wasn't a sadder sight I could ever imagine. Clouds drifted high above, blocked the sun and for a few seconds turned the day as dark as my feelings were. When the sun returned and bathed the stick of lumber with his name on it in its glaring unforgiving light, I realized I wasn't going to get the relief I craved; not here; not in the cemetery. I got back into the car.

Someone beside the woman from the cemetery office told me a visitor usually left rocks to let the soul of the departed one know that it could rest more easily because it hadn't been forgotten. I didn't believe any of that religious stuff, but something got me out of the car. I picked up a few rocks and stacked them neatly in the fresh dirt alongside the grave marker and put a few on my grandmother's grave as well. I looked at several near-by graves and saw that there were stones on several of the headstones. There was no gravestone to mark my grandfather's grave yet. The rocks in the dirt would have to do. I got back into the car; it took me twice as long to get out of the cemetery as it had getting to the grave site. I felt like shit as I finally drove away from the cemetery.

chapter 2

Sam's Story

Sam Brandeis walked home quickly from the Sabbath Service. He spoke to several men but he cut every conversation as short as he could. The streets of the *shtetl* were alive with men after the morning services. Stories of the week were exchanged and general news of the area was discussed. The Rabbi's plea for safety in the *shtetl* was also discussed, with many of the men believing that it was not strong enough. There were several men who expressed the desire to locate guns to fight the Cossacks with.

Sam had made up his mind and he knew he had to talk to his wife before his resolve weakened or she could mount more objections to his plans. He knew she would be standing at the door holding Mildred in her arms waiting for him.

Eva made him promise that he would speak to the Rabbi before he made a final decision. He didn't like breaking his word to her, but he knew he wouldn't speak to anyone about the decision, not this decision. There was no more time in his mind for reasoning and debating, for talking to the Rabbi or anyone else. He and Luca Steiner had made up their minds days ago, after the last Cossack horse had disappeared into the night. They shook hands and pledged absolute silence.

Eva was standing at the door as he supposed she would be. He held his finger to his lips after he said "good Sabbath" to her and kissed the baby.

"Tonight, Eva, we leave. No more talking; no more words; no more promises from the Rabbi; we're leaving when the sun goes down. Get ready. Sunset, the Sabbath is over, we go. Those damned Cossacks take a special joy killing and raping Jews. Not another day or night here with raping and killing. We've made our last prayer to God on this Sabbath from this *shtetl*, Eva. We speak to no one; the sun goes down, the Sabbath ends, we pack up and we go."

Sam Brandeis turned from his wife before she could utter a word. He walked toward Luca's home. They met in the middle of the dirt street closest to Luca's home. Each man stared at the other; then they came close to each other, moved their taluses out of the way and embraced.

"Brandeis, our day has arrived."

"Steiner, it has arrived, finally."

Neither of them could remember how or when they began calling each other by their last names rather than their first names. That was how it was with them and only them in the *shtetl*.

"No more in that hole they call a cellar. The rats have taken their last bite out of me, Steiner. My little girl can't take it and Eva will lose another baby if we have to spend one more night hiding from those bastards. Today was our last Sabbath in the synagogue, Steiner. I prayed hard and I know you did too. Not another word to discuss or go over; we're gone for good."

"Immediately when the sun goes down ending the Sabbath, we're gone, Brandeis. Whatever is, for better or worse, we go; you with Eva and Miriam, I go with Rachel. I added a prayer to God to make the weather good. Let's go to the cellar for one last look around and make sure we've packed everything we need and want."

"You know Steiner, during that last raid I know I 'heard' some Cossacks yelling that weren't Cossacks. They were yelling their curses in Polish."

"You heard them too? I know they were Poles. They were not even in uniforms, Brandeis. I peeked out of the cellar and I saw them too. It's not long before they'll be at our doors pulling our wives out into the streets to rape them and then kill our children. God only knows what's next."

"It's good we're leaving."

Luca found a clearing in the forest several miles from their town where they could all sleep for one night, hidden from any discovery. He explained to Sam that it would be easy for them if the weather cooperated. Sam agreed with him.

"You followed exactly where we went? If anything happens you can get there with Eva and Miriam?"

"If you're asking me if I can find this place by myself, the answer is yes."

"Good."

"You know, Brandeis, we're one of the lucky families who will travel all together, if we can afford the steerage."

"You're right, Steiner. We have just about enough to bring them with us."

"It is because our fathers were smart enough to save a little while we starved a lot."

"We won't have to leave our families here and then send for them like most of the others."

The two men walked slowly in the direction of the cellar. They avoided as many men in the street as they could until they arrived at the cellar, located about fifty yards behind their homes. Luca and Sam went into the cellar to take what they wanted to keep for their journey. Luca went to the far corner where he and Rachel lay hidden until they heard the horses leaving, indicating that a p*ogrom* was over for that night. Their place was across from where Sam and Eva lay hidden with their daughter Mildred. They remained separated so that in case one family was found, the other one might not be detected, especially if the Cossacks who found them would be satisfied that they had enough to rape and kill for one night.

Luca pulled some canvas away from one pile of his and Rachel's things. He pulled out an odd-shaped box. He brushed it off and handed it to Sam. Sam turned it over in his hands and handed it back to Luca.

"What is it?"

"It's a special box, Brandeis. I told you about the man who was supposed to be my uncle Leopold."

"I remember; your uncle, the one who is in the Kaiser's Army?"

"That's him, Leopold Kalina. Not really a relative, certainly not a real relation, but he's been "uncle" to me all my life. I don't know how or when or why he became "uncle" but that's what I always called him. He never came to the *shtetl*. We visited him in Vilna where he has an estate, once every year. One year, he gave me this box. I think it was for Christmas, certainly not for Chanukah; I think it must have been for Christmas. He used to carry his gun and some bullets in that box whenever he went on some kind of maneuvers. I have seen pictures of him on his horse, holding the box in one hand. Look here, Brandeis."

Luca pressed a small lever on the top of the box and

it sprang open. The box was empty. On the bottom of the box his name was printed:

L-E-O-P-O-L-D K-A-L-I-N-A
LIEUTENANT in the
A-R-M-Y of the K-A-I-S-E-R

On each side of the box was a Polish Flag in full color.

"Now listen to me Brandeis. No arguments, no speeches, just listen."

"Sure, Luca. I'm listening."

"If anything happens to me while we're traveling, anything that stops me from continuing with you and Eva, I want you to take this box and Rachel and get to where we planned to go, where we know there is still steerage available to America for a price we can afford."

"What could happen to you, Steiner?"

"I don't know, Brandeis, but if you have trouble and I'm not there, show them the box."

"Who?"

"Whoever stops you. Anyone in uniform who stops you will know the name in the box and, of course, they'll know the flag."

"Nothing is going to happen to you Steiner that does not happen to me."

"Brandeis, the box is like a passport if you are stopped. Just keep telling anyone in uniform that

General Leopold Kalina of Vilna is your uncle. He's not my uncle so he might as well not be your uncle either. If you have to, dare them to call him about his "nephew" Luca Steiner. The last time I saw my "uncle" Leopold Kalina, he told me I should use the box if I got into a scrape with a soldier or a policeman.

"He said, 'Luca, you don't have to tell your mother. Just show them the box'."

"I don't understand, Steiner."

"You don't have to understand; sometimes, you're a pain in the neck, Sam Brandeis. For once in your life, don't understand, just please do what I tell you to do."

"Steiner, all I know is that if anything happens to you, it will happen to me, too."

"Sam Brandeis, stop being so damned stubborn. Do what I say, not what you think."

"Hey, Steiner take it easy. Okay, I'll do what you say. It does no harm to agree because nothing will happen to us, or our wives or my child."

"Brandeis, all the names and addresses of the organizations who can help us in America when we land will be in this box. I am putting them there."

Sam watched as Luca stuffed all the information they had gathered about landing in America and a place called Ellis Island, where they knew they would be taken.

"Here, Steiner, put the name of my cousin Mordecai,

the mentch, who knows we are coming to America. He will know what we're supposed to do and where we're supposed to go."

Luca took the paper his friend handed to him with a name and an address on it and stuffed it into the box along with all the other papers.

"Everything we will need, Brandeis, when we arrive in America."

The two men went over the piles of their needs that they knew they would take on their journey that night. Everything was tightly packed so as to make their bundles easier to carry. Luca shoved the box back into the bag he had pulled it from. Luca's wife, Rachel, was a large, strong woman and she had agreed with Eva that she would help to carry whatever Eva's baby needed to have every day. Eva's current pregnancy had held Sam back several days after the last pogrom before he knew he had to make final plans with Luca.

"The new baby will be twice as strong when it's born, if it can survive the forest and the ocean, Steiner. I worry about Eva's strength, but if we stay here, we'll all be dead. We must trust God to watch over us."

"I will knock three short on your door when the sun is down and the Sabbath is over, Brandeis. When Rachel reaches the cellar door, I'll knock once. Be ready."

"I'm ready now. We'll all be there, Steiner. See you later."

After the three knocks on the door, as darkness fell, one knock followed and the two families met and disappeared into the woods behind the *shtetl*.

Luca led them directly to the clearing he found. They secured their bundles underneath the brush and they settled as comfortably as they could on the unforgiving ground. The baby slept but the four adults stayed awake and talked for almost the entire night.

They ate sparingly; only food that didn't have to be cooked; no fires unless there was a dire emergency.

"No fires for food except a tiny spark if we have to warm something for Mildred," was what they had agreed upon. Eva breast fed her daughter so there was not a need for any fires. They were packed and walking as the sun rose.

"Anyone gets tired," Luca said, "call out and we will rest for a while. There is no need to hurry. If we stay away from the main roads and keep walking in the forest, the chances are we will not run into any soldiers who will demand to know what we are doing in the forest and where we are going. We don't need questions we cannot answer."

On the evening of the fourth day, the forest path they were on ended at the banks of a river. Sam and Luca unpacked all their bundles and put them against the trees. They told their wives to stay hidden as well as they could. Then the two men went to the river and sat on the rocks at the bank of the river. Sam pulled out the rough map they had drawn before they left the *shtetl*. He pointed to the marking on the map that indicated the water they had arrived at.

"Here, Steiner, we are here."

Sam traced the thin line on their rough map that was supposed to be the river.

"We have done well, Steiner. It's only four days and nights and we are close to the German city that still had steerage available when we left the *shtetl*. We have to get across the river safely and we'll be in Germany. Then a few more days and we'll be there."

"Those days should be far easier for us, Brandeis. The Germans don't give two damns for poor Jews wandering the streets. I'm sure, if we have to, we can find a Jewish family in the town that will be a little bit friendly to us. As long as we don't beg for anything, we'll be okay until we get to the waterfront where the big ocean liners are. We can only hope we don't have to wait too long to buy steerage on one of them for all of us."

"We agreed if we had to buy steerage on separate boats, we would do that. We can meet in America, in New York, Steiner."

"That sounds good, Brandeis, so good, I can hardly believe it."

The men went back to where their wives were still waiting at the edge of the forest. They showed them their map and explained how close they were to being in Germany and how much safer they would be than they had been for the last four days and nights. The two women had smiles on their dirty, worn faces for the first time in days. Eva held Mildred up toward the sky then she pointed the baby towards the river.

"Little girl, our Mildred, soon, soon baby, we'll be sailing to America," she crooned. She put the baby on a blanket. The four adults held hands tightly, formed a circle and did an abbreviated imitation of a *hora*.

"God willing, soon we will be free."

"How will we cross the water?"

"In the morning before you get up I'll go," Luca said, "and find the shallowest place in the water. Then we will wade across. If it is too deep, we will go one at a time. Brandeis and I will get Rachel, Eva and Miriam to the other side. We will come back for our bundles. If we have to swim, we will swim. If we have to carry each of you, we will carry each of you. We will dry ourselves and our clothes and find a road to the city."

The sky started to lighten the next morning when Sam was awakened by a sharp, crackling sound. As he became fully awake, he sat up and looked for Luca; it took him several seconds to realize that Luca Steiner was not there. Suddenly Sam knew that what had awakened him was a gun shot.

He sprang up and ran to the bank of the river.

He ran along the bank until he saw Luca in the water struggling to get to land. Fear gripped Sam as he saw blood running into the water from Luca's body. Sam jumped into the river and when he got to Luca he saw the blood was running from a wound in Luca's chest. Sam pulled him out of the water and Luca fell in a heap on the rocks alongside the river. Sam saw that Luca was trying to say something. He got on his knees and put his ear to Luca's mouth.

"Brandeis, take Rachel, Eva and the baby and the box and get back into the woods, quickly," Sam heard the hoarse whisper that came from the dying Luca.

"Steiner, I will pull you behind the trees. No one will see you from there."

"Brandeis, I'm done. Take Rachel, your family and the box and get back into the trees. Wait there until it is dark again, then cross the river where you found me. It is the closest and shallowest spot from here."

Luca's whisper trailed off and then stopped. His face turned and his cheek touched the ground. Sam looked at his friend and knew that life had ebbed from Luca Steiner; he was dead. He pulled the body into the trees away from where both women had already awakened. When Rachel saw Sam pulling a body, she screamed, ran to where Sam was and fell screaming upon Luca's body.

"Eva, go to Rachel and try to keep her quiet. If she has to scream, get her further back into the trees. Eva,

17

there is no help for Luca; he's dead. Keep Rachel quiet or it will be death for us all."

Sam picked up his daughter and put her back on her blanket as far away from the river as he could. He went back for all their belongings and piled them alongside the baby. He went to Eva's side and helped pull Rachel away from Luca's body. Sam put his hand over Rachel's mouth and managed to stifle the screams coming from her throat; it was inhuman; the most dreadful sound he had ever heard.

"Eva, take Rachel and Mildred into the trees, far, far back into the trees. Pull Rachel, if you have to. When she stops screaming, and can understand what you are saying, try to tell her I will take care of Luca as best I can. Tell her I will pray for him and us. And tell her I will bring her to Luca's grave, whatever and wherever it may be, when she is able to go to where he will be lying. And Eva, whoever did this to Luca Steiner might still be here someplace. Remember, as little noise as possible. I'll be back as soon as I can. Eva, no noise, none. Our lives depend on it."

Tears were streaming down his wife's face when Sam left her to deal with Rachel Steiner. He heard muffled sobs from the women as he left to try to bury his friend's body. His entire body was racked with pain and sobs as he walked through the trees to where he had left Luca Steiner's body.

He searched the shore line for at least a mile in each direction. He stopped to listen for noise in the forest, but he couldn't hear any. He understood that whoever killed Luca might still be somewhere close by.

When he was sure he was alone, he returned to where he left Luca Steiner's body. It took him a long time to dig a ditch with his hands and a spoon that was long enough to hold Luca Steiner's body. Sam dragged the dead body and placed it in the ditch as lovingly as he could. He covered Luca Steiner with the dirt he had dug up and some branches and leaves. He covered the site with rocks. He stood and said the Hebrew prayer for the dead; he went back into the forest to find where Eva, Rachel and his baby were hidden.

When Sam returned, Rachel handed him the box Luca told her to give to Sam Brandeis, just "in case".

"Eva," Sam said to his wife, "we will stay hidden here for a few days while Rachel deals with what happened to Luca. I have no way of knowing if there are people in the forest that hunt Jews for sport. Please hide the box; we mustn't lose it at all costs. We must remain hidden as well as we can. Luca would have wanted us to keep going. We must get out of the forest and to the ocean."

Sam turned to Rachel.

"Rachel, when you are ready, I will take you to where I put Luca in the ground. I don't know about us sitting *shiva*, but we will stay here as long as we can. If we can keep ourselves safe from killers and live here among God's trees, maybe we can all sit *shiva* the correct amount of time. You must be honest and tell me when you are ready to leave to get to a boat to buy steerage for America."

"Sam, I am not your responsibility."

"You are not a responsibility, Rachel. You are a traveler going to America. You are going with your family. We are your family; you are our family. For now, you are Eva's cousin. We happen to be going in the same direction to the same place therefore we are a family, one family. There is no question of responsibility. We are one family from now on."

Sam reached out for Rachel and pressed her tightly to his body. He felt her sobs and he heard sorrowful noises coming from deep within her massive frame. Eva put a blanket on a bed of leaves and put Mildred on her blanket. She came to where her husband and Rachel were standing. She put her arms around the two of them. A mournful wail came from Eva as she held her husband and her friend. The depths of their sorrow echoed through the tall trees. Words they all knew far too well from the prayer for the dead in Hebrew were on their lips.

chapter 3

My story

BY THE TIME I WAS ready for my next trip to the cemetery, three days later, my automobile's navigation system to the cemetery had been completely destroyed. It was now my responsibility to pay full attention to the traffic and all the insane curves on the Inter-Boro Parkway. I was more convinced than ever that this particular parkway had been designed by an escapee from a lunatic asylum to get some form of revenge on unsuspecting drivers, because he or she probably failed their driver's test at least 10 times.

This day was not like the first day I went there alone. The sun was nowhere to be seen; it was raining steadily, a downpour that seemed to come in sheets rather than in drops.

The same woman from the office accosted me again. This time she was under a large umbrella. She had to lean closer to the driver's side window I opened because of the umbrella's expanse. I had to roll it all the way down to hear what she said. Not only had she forgotten how to smile, her breath was an amalgamation of foul-smelling odors punctuated by the rain which somehow managed to hit me in the face.

"I remember you," she said leaning into the opened window. "You're the one who doesn't want a Rabbi."

"That's me, no Rabbi."

"Did you leave stones like I told you to?"

"Yes Ma'am, I did."

"At least you got that right."

She turned, forgot to ask me if I knew where I was going, and hurried back into the office. Maybe she assumed the car still knew where it had to go. It could even be that she was the witch who had refigured my car's directional system; I had heard that strange things happen to people who work in cemeteries.

I drove to the grave site. The rain was coming down even harder by the time I got there. I rolled down the passenger's side window again and sat quietly as the rain continued. The name printed on the stick jammed into the ground did not run from the downpour. It seemed to be staring at me to force me to get out of the car. I opened the door. The dirt that had been piled on the grave sank into a muddy pool. The water from the rain drained from the pile of dirt making a small river that encircled the entire grave.

There had been no release for me from my sadness. It made no sense to me to get out of the car. I closed the door and sat for a few minutes. Nothing occurred. I decided there was no sense getting out in order to put some stones on the muddy pile. I drove away and stopped at the door that the woman had disappeared behind. I found her office. I knocked on the door and, when there was no sound beyond the door, I opened it. She was seated behind a metal desk piled with papers. She did not look up when I entered.

"Please, ma'am, can you tell me when the gravestone for Samuel Brandeis will be put in place?"

"I don't have that information sir. You'll have to check with whoever you hired to make it. They'll know when it is ready, which they should have told you by now. When they advise us, someone in your family will be notified."

"Thank you."

The office smelled more than she did.

I drove out of the cemetery. I made myself a promise to return the next time the sun shone even though I had to get back on that insane parkway at least several more times to do so.

Two days later, the sun reappeared and I was able to keep my promise to myself. I started out after I was sure the early morning traffic had eased. The insane curves on the parkway were still the same and the unerring ability of my car to navigate almost on its own had not returned.

After a very slow drive, I entered the cemetery and I stopped at the office once more. The woman approached the car. When she saw that it was me, she waved me on.

"You're a veteran visitor by now, still without a Rabbi," I heard her shout as I drove away.

The dirt piled on the site had been flattened out; I assumed it was from the torrential rain a few days before. Small indentations and depressions were left in the dirt where the rain had continually run off during the storm.

I got out of the car and stood by Sam Brandeis' grave. Memories flashed through my mind of the love I had known from him all my life. Tears welled up and started down my cheeks. Before I realized it, I was sobbing aloud. It took me several minutes to bring my sobs under control. As I bent to find some rocks, I heard a voice. I looked up; there was no one there. I picked up several rocks; I heard the voice again. I looked up again. Peeking out from behind a cloud that looked like a small dog, there was Sam Brandeis' smiling face, beaming down on me.

"Sonny, it's OK," the voice said. "Crying is allowed in this place where they put me and you have come. I'm here too, and it is okay. Not to worry. I don't need your tears, but it is a good idea to get rid of them, once and for all. There are a few things here that need a hammer and some nails, not tears. Tears don't work good here, but it's a good place to get rid of all of them."

When I heard that voice speak of a "hammer and nails", the grief began to lift from my being. I wiped my eyes and looked up at the 'dog-cloud' but Sam Brandeis was gone, probably forever.

The Jewish religion, among numerous other invocations, pontificates that the soul of the deceased needs a year before it is ready to rise to its final resting place, presumably in heaven. There was, of course a service for that, too. I didn't know where my grandfather's soul had gone; I knew it wasn't a year since he died. If there was something wherever he was that needed fixing, that's where he could be found, soul and hammer and nails. That thought brought me back to the midnight I had driven him to the hospital after talking to the doctor. As he was lifted from his bed, he called to me.

"*Pitchela Richela*, (his pet name for me), the oxygen tent is no good. It should be adjusted so that the cold air should not blow up my sleeve. When I get better, I'll fix it so that the next man who needs it won't be so cold."

I didn't know then and I still don't know whether that was an indication of his body surrendering to the inevitable. He had taken the time to speak to me of a needed repair as he had so many, many times before.

Now, I knew that his face beaming at me and my being able to hear the sound of his voice, whether real or imagined, had brought me to the beginnings of a finality to my grief and to my whole being.

I put a few more rocks on top of the dirt. I left the cemetery, a sadder man and hopefully a wiser one than when I had arrived; certainly a changed man. I left with several more questions than I had arrived with; perhaps never to be answered questions, but still questions that remained with me.

chapter 4

Sam's Story

SAM CLIMBED OVER BODIES UNTIL he reached Eva and Rachel. He hated to descend back down into the steerage after being on the deck of the ship for twenty minutes of fresh air, but when he saw where the ship was, he knew he had to go down into the blistering heat and the revolting stink in the hull to get them.

"Come and see; come and see where we are, both of you. The notes I made in my little book were accurate; we're here."

Eva held the baby and Sam pulled the two women up to the deck. A glorious morning was breaking in New York and the ship was gliding slowly into the harbor, past the Statue of Liberty.

"Hold Mildred high up, Eva, and show her our new home, New York. Show our baby the Statue; It's America; Eva, Rachel, Miriam, it's the dream."

Two robust blasts from the ship's horn and in a few

minutes the steerage of the ship emptied of its human cargo and the deck was filled with shoving people straining to see New York's shores.

The nightmare that was Ellis Island and entry into the United States dismayed many arrivals. There were shouts of disapproval. Disappointment and doubts were voiced by the arriving immigrants as if an army of Russian Cossacks awaited them in the stifling, airless building ready to begin another pogrom.

The lines that had been set up between rope barriers were long and the progress torturously slow. It took the efforts of many volunteers from the organizations that were there to help calm the new arrivals. Fears and terrors had to be allayed; their trip of weeks of almost prisonlike conditions they endured in the steerage of the ship that brought them made assurances of safety more and more difficult. Some of the newcomers fainted, others shrieked and screamed.

Sam, Eva and Rachel took turns holding the baby. Sam constantly checked his writing in the notebook and he finally saw a sign that had the name of one of the organizations he had scribbled in his notebook.

"Hold the baby. There's the name of the organization, there hanging from the ceiling; it's in my book. I'll go; you wait here with the baby and Rachel. I'll bring someone back with me. Give me the box Luca left for us. All the information is in it."

Sam put the box under his arm, crawled under the rope barrier and forced his way toward the desk beneath the sign of the organization. His hat fell off; he left it where it fell. He didn't want to lose sight of the organization listed in his book. He was afraid that it might disappear and he wouldn't be able to find it again.

When he reached the desk under the sign, he opened the box and pulled out all the papers he and Luca had stuffed into it.

"You must wait your turn, sir. Please stand over here."

"I'm good at waiting my turn. Since I left the old country, I've been waiting. I'll wait some more."

Sam turned to make sure he could see Eva in the massive crowd of humanity behind him. He waved and when he couldn't attract her attention, he called out her name. Rachel heard him and she waved.

"That's my family," he said to the woman behind the desk.

"They're not going anywhere, sir. They'll be all right where they are now. We need some information from you. It's slow, but we'll get it all done. We always manage."

"Would it be all right if I went back to get my hat while I'm waiting? It came off when I ran to your desk."

"Of course."

"I won't lose my place?"

"No, you won't. There are three ahead of you. I'll remember your place."

Sam found his hat crushed and filthy after having been trod on by many feet. He brushed it off, tried to return it to its original shape, put it on his head and returned to the desk.

"I'm back."

"I can see that. I saved your place. There are now only two before it's your turn."

When Sam was able to announce his "first on line", he shouted to Eva and Rachel to join him on the line. Then he pulled a worn, wrinkled piece of yellow paper from the box. He handed it to the woman behind the desk.

"This paper says Mordecai. I can't read the last name. Do you know what it is?"

"Yes. Eva, your cousin's name is Mordecai Levy. It is Levy?"

"His name is Levy. Mordecai Levy. You know that Sam."

The woman behind the desk looked up and saw tears streaming down Rachel Steiner's cheeks.

"Are you all right?'

"She's OK. Not to worry," Sam said.

Eva handed the baby to her husband and leaned over the desk to speak in private to the woman there.

"Her man is *geshtorben*."

"Luca Steiner died on the trip," Sam interrupted his wife. "Rachel is still very, very sad, still mourning."

The woman behind the desk sensed something terrible had happened to the woman with the tearful cheeks. She decided she'd better continue and not ask any questions that didn't have anything to do with the immigrant's entry into the United States.

"Ah yes, Levy. I can see it. And under the name is an address on Hester Street. Is that right?"

Sam leaned over and stared at the paper.

"Hester Street is what it says; Mordecai Levy from Hester Street. That's my wife's cousin and that's where he lives. On that street."

"There has been a man named Mordecai Levy here every day for a week. He has been asking for the Brandeis family and waiting for the ship to arrive. You are Brandeis?"

"I am Samuel Brandeis. This is my wife Eva Brandeis and this is my daughter, Mildred Brandeis," Sam said proudly.

"The poor woman with the tears is Rachel Steiner. She is now part of our family," Sam said.

Sam took the box from Rachel Steiner and showed it to the woman behind the desk. He pressed the lever on the top of the box. The lid flew open and everything he had stuffed in it flew out.

"I'll pick it all up, the papers. You look at the name

on the bottom of the box. As Sam picked up what had fallen out of the box, the woman looked inside.

"Leopold Kalina of the Kaiser's Army," the woman read aloud. "That doesn't matter here in America."

Sam showed her the name again.

"Here, in this box is a name. You can see the name in this box. It was very important in Germany when we were stopped and questioned. We were very frightened but after they saw the name on the bottom of the box and who that name represented, there were no more questions. Whoever saw on the bottom of the box was very impressed and we were let go to go wherever we were going. Do you have to see the box, too?"

"No, here in America you don't need a box to be welcomed. Put it away and keep it as a souvenir of your safe arrival in New York."

"That's good. I worried all the way here it wouldn't work."

"Mordecai Levy will be here today, I'm sure. By the time we finish with the filling out and the examining, Mordecai Levy will show up. I know it."

"Examining?"

"We must check all those who arrive to make sure they are healthy and not carrying any diseases. It is not difficult. You are not to be frightened or worry."

"We are all fine and healthy."

"The examinations are done by doctors. Please,

don't be worried. Now some questions and after that the examinations. By that time your cousin, Mordecai Levy will be here."

Mordecai brought Sam Brandeis, his wife Eva carrying Miriam and Rachel Steiner to Hester Street. His visitors had never in their lives experienced anything like Hester Street. The crowds of people overwhelmed them; the activities on the street were a never-ending pool of commotion of scrambling men, women and children. The noise of humanity and traffic in each neighborhood they walked through left each of them wondering where in the world had they come to.

As they walked, Mordecai spoke quietly to his cousin Eva in Yiddish.

"It is good you are finally here with your husband and baby. Who is the woman with you?"

Eva explained the tortuous details of Luca's death as best she could.

"She is part of our family now, Mordecai."

"I have rented rooms for you in the same building where I live on Hester Street. I don't know if the landlord will let another adult live in the apartment. I am not even sure there is room for another person in the apartment."

"We will have to make do, Mordecai. We cannot leave her alone; it is a new country for her, too. It would not be right. Sam will speak to the landlord. If we have to make another arrangement, we will have to make another arrangement. Rachel Steiner is part of our family now. That is the way it is, Mordecai."

"I hear what you are saying, my cousin. We will do whatever we have to do."

"Thank you, Mordecai."

"I found a job for Sam. You wrote he can build anything. The job is with a friend, a carpenter. Sam will have to make an arrangement for the salary with my friend. I hope it will be enough for all of you to live on."

"I'm sure when we are moved in, Rachel will find work. She will not allow us to pay for her unless she helps out."

"Can she sew?"

"She can sew."

"There is work in a factory not too far from the apartment. She can walk there."

"Thank you again, Mordecai. Everything is settled."

chapter 5

Sam's Story

THE ROOMS THEY LIVED IN on Hester Street were cramped, but, as there was a limited choice, there were few, if any, complaints about sleeping conditions. Eva and Rachel scrubbed as much of the dirt away as they could, erasing the memory of another poor family with their elbow grease.

Sam was employed by the carpenter Mordecai had recommended him to and Rachel was able to secure a position in a factory that made shirtwaists on Greene Street, close to the East River. They never had enough money to purchase anything remotely resembling luxuries, but with Eva in charge of the money, the family was able to eat enough, pay the rent and barely get through every month.

Their landlord was a small, wizened little man, who managed to leave the pungent aura of garlic ahead of him and behind him, wherever his person happened to walk. His name was Benjamin Krinsky, but behind his foul smelling back the tenants all called him "shy, shy". It was an abbreviation for "Shylock the shyster". One of them thought up the name but they used the abbreviation whenever he was in earshot.

The only time Eva looked at him was when he banged on their door on the first of every month to collect the rent. The Brandeis family lived on the fourth floor of the tenement. Eva kept the apartment door opened a crack on the first of the month so she could hear the other tenants complaining to him and know how long it would be before he would be knocking on her door. She always held the rent tightly in her hand until Mr. Krinsky arrived on the fourth floor. When he knocked, she stuck her hand out with the money in it. Sam put a chain on the door. When it was in place, the door could only be opened a small crack, not nearly wide enough for a man to enter the apartment.

Sometimes a tenant had to beg him for a few extra days to pay the rent. Eva learned that he would push his way into the apartment of any tenant where the rent was going to be late. She heard from some of the women tenants that if they were going to be late, he would try to take liberties with them. A lot of them wore their heaviest coats when they knew they would have to beg for a few extra days.

When the Brandeis family moved in the little man

made special note of Rachel Steiner. Sam Brandeis said she was a cousin who decided at the last minute to come with him and Eva. Benjamin Krinsky knew Rachel wasn't a relation, but he kept quiet. He had plans for such a strong, good- looking woman. He touched her arm and then her shoulder before he would agree to put a cot in the apartment.

"That's extra," he said. "I did not know there was to be another woman living here. You'll need to give another quarter."

"I will when the cot arrives," Sam said.

"There may be another way, Brandeis. You should talk to Rachel, your cousin."

"I'm not interested in any other way, Benny. Another quarter when the cot arrives, not before."

"From now on, every month, Brandeis."

"Every month, Benny, after the cot arrives."

When Rachel found work in the factory, Sam walked her there in the morning and tried to pick her up on his way home if he finished his work at the carpenter's in time. Once he was early; he walked up several flights of stairs until he saw Rachel with her head bent over her sewing. Sam had not realized that there was machinery in the factory.

On their way home that night, Sam asked Rachel questions about the machines in the factory. He told Rachel the next time he was early, he would speak to the man in charge. When he was early Sam carried a small can of oil with him, together with pliers and a screw driver. He found Rachel at her machine. She pointed out the man in charge. Sam offered to keep the machinery in better working order. The man followed Sam throughout the factory as Sam put oil on the parts of each machine that needed it. He also adjusted a part or two on a machine so that it would run faster. He stayed with Sam as he made adjustments to several machines. Sam demonstrated that under his care every machine would not only run smoother and quieter, but faster, so it could produce more shirt waists at no extra cost, except for the small amount he would require for his services. The man in charge and Sam struck an agreement. Sam would come to the factory several times a week after the rest of the help went home and take care of the machines. There were many times that the women worked very late. Sam would wait until their machines were turned off so he could work on them and keep them working smoothly and quickly. He put aside every nickel he could.

Sam's employer was Jewish and so it was no effort for Sam to make an arrangement that did not include working on Saturdays. The shop was closed on Saturdays anyway. He made up any missed time by arriving early.

"That day,Shabbas," (Saturday) Sam said, "is reserved for God."

"You are right, his boss said. This shop is closed on Saturday. This is America, but we must not forget who we are and where we came from. We will work Sundays if we have the business. Do what you want, it's your Saturday. Just change your schedule and from now on, you come to work on Sundays, Sam."

Sam went to synagogue for services on Saturday mornings and again on Saturday evenings. He did not go to where Rachel worked on Saturdays to walk her home.

He came in contact with many small business owners where he worked. It seemed they always needed "a minor repair" or "a small addition" to something in their places of businesses. Everything they needed was always dictated by the price Sam's boss would charge for his labor. Sam quickly came to the realization that he was very important to the man who had hired him.

One of the men Sam met and liked was Schlomo Bernstein. They realized that the shtetls they came from were very near each other. Schlomo Bernstein lived only a block from where Sam lived on Hester Street. When they had time, they talked about where they came from. They realized that the shtetls they left were less than a mile from each other. They mentioned names of people they knew in the shtetls and found there were several they each knew. They talked freely of their dreams here in America.

"Brandeis, did you ever think of leaving here and going out for yourself?"

"I think and think, Bernstein. I'm not ready yet."

"If you wait until you're ready, Brandeis, you'll die here."

"No, Bernstein. I'll die, but not here."

"Brandeis, I have a mattress store in Brooklyn. I make mattresses and pillows and I sell them. It does all right for me and my wife. We have no children so there is enough for both of us."

"Bernstein, what I know about mattresses and pillows you could fall asleep on."

"A good joke, Brandeis, but I'm thinking of making box springs to go with my mattresses and pillows. You could learn to make box springs, Brandeis. We could put the mattresses on the box springs and sell them as a unit. A customer could transact the whole sleeping business in one shot. We could both make a good living."

"How long does it take you to get to your store in Brooklyn, Bernstein?"

"About an hour."

"I walk Rachel to the factory and I'm at my job in less than half-an-hour, and that's free without any carfare. An hour is a long time and costs more than walking, Bernstein."

"For your own business, it is worth it, Brandeis. Me and my wife have looked at apartments in Brooklyn.

Not bad; better than in Hester Street, let me tell you. You don't have to make up your mind now, but don't let it disappear from your thoughts."

"You know I won't, Bernstein. A funny thing Bernstein, my best friend in the shtetl's name was Luca Steiner. He always called me Brandeis and I always called him Steiner. You and me, we're using only last names, also."

"Maybe it's important, Brandeis. Maybe it means we'll be partners one day, Brandeis. B & B, Bedding. The three B's. I could think of worse names."

"Maybe it is, Bernstein, maybe it is."

"Brandeis, we will talk more, I promise you."

On a warm, sunny Saturday in June, early in the evening, Sam heard banging on his door. It was several weeks after he had spoken to Schlomo Bernstein. He usually rested after the services. He was lying on his bed. Eva was out with Mildred. The banging on the door continued.

Sam got up; he put the chain on the door and opened it a crack. The landlord, Benjamin Krinsky stood there with tears streaming down his face.

"Sam, there's a terrible fire. It's the Triangle Shirtwaist Factory on Greene Street that's on fire. Your cousin Rachel, she works there, doesn't she?"

"My God, Benny, she does."

"It's a terrible fire, Sam. You better get down there."

"If you see my wife, please tell her what happened and tell her to stay away from the factory. If you don't find her, I'll be home as soon as I can. Thanks."

Sam could see black smoke billowing in the sky as he ran toward the fire. There were thick, heavy ropes, reminiscent of those at Ellis Island around the entire block. The badly burned bodies of the dead women workers from the factory were strewn along the pier. Relatives searched the bodies screaming names and looking for their loved ones.

Sam slipped under one of the ropes and tried to get to the one door he could see. The smoke was far too heavy for him and in a few seconds he couldn't see anything, not even the building.

Sam ran back under the ropes and wiped his eyes. He finally spotted Eva pushing Mildred's carriage in the street among the smoking ruins. He ran towards her. She screamed and dropped to her knees.

"It's Rachel, Sam. This was our Rachel. She has no face, Sam."

"Eva, please come away from there. Take the baby and go home. I'll tell you as soon as I know."

She pulled away from her husband's grasp.

"Sam, that's Rachel. She's dead, Sam. Our Rachel is dead, burned up."

Eva pointed to a body covered with a dirty sheet. Sam grabbed the handle of the baby carriage and walked it a few feet away from the fire and toward Hester Street. Eva went back to where the body of Rachel Steiner lay smoldering under a dirty sheet.

Sam's eyes were tearing; he could hardly see his wife. He found her on her knees again, next to the body under the blanket, screaming Rachel's name.

"Eva, we must get Mildred out of here. She will choke on the smoke. Come, get up. You cannot help Rachel anymore. We must get out of here and away from all this smoke. Only the smell reached Hester Street. We must go back to Hester Street. Get up, Eva, get up. The walls will collapse and Mildred and you will get hurt. Now, Eva, now. Move now, Eva!"

Eva took her coat off, laid it across Rachel's body and moved away and toward her husband and her baby. Sam retrieved the coat and pushed Eva and the carriage away from the fire.

Out of roughly 275 girls and women who worked in the factory, 145 died that night in the fire. They died from suffocation, smoke inhalation, barred doors that would not open, jumping to safety out of the windows and down the elevator shaft. In some instances the crush of bodies fleeing was also a cause of death as the steps overflowed with the bodies of women who tripped in their desperation trying to escape the searing flames.

Sam Brandeis joined the International Ladies Garment Workers Union. He carried signs written in

Hebrew, scrawled in Yiddish and also in English, urging that the owners of the Triangle Shirtwaist Factory be dragged unto court, tried and punished for their negligence. He marched in Brooklyn and Manhattan urging new- comers to their new country to join in the Union's fight for the worker. He was solidly dependable to be a part of almost every picket line and Protest March he could. He refused to accept a higher position in the Union because he believed that he would no longer remain a 'worker' but would become a 'boss' owning his own business and not able to work toward the worker's equality in that manner.

It took Eva several weeks to begin to recover from the death of her friend and the memories of that terrible night. She wouldn't leave the apartment without Sam as she was paralyzed by the thought of being alone outside. Sam walked the baby as much as he could. Every day in the apartment on Hester Street was a terrible ordeal for her.

It was then that Sam Brandeis began to give serious thought to Schlomo Bernstein's proposal. There were too many memories of Rachel in their apartment and on the streets of the neighborhood. The constant talk about the fire and who was lost in it continued unabated. Eva could find no peace for herself anywhere.

He spoke to Schlomo again. Using the time that he used to spend at the Triangle Factory, Sam went to one of Schlomo's suppliers to watch and learn the process of making a box spring. The steel springs were unwieldy at first and the rough string used to tie the springs together made blisters on his hands that often bled. He bought thick gloves. When the bleeding finally ceased, Schlomo pronounced Sam ready for serious box spring making and their partnership.

When Eva told Sam she thought she had lost their second baby, Sam's mind was made up.

"You'll go to the doctor, Eva. No guessing about this. Go to a doctor and make sure."

"I'm sure, Sam."

"Go to a doctor anyway, Eva."

A neighborhood doctor confirmed Eva's worse thoughts. He did what he could to make sure there would be no infection or any other damage done to Eva.

"Eva, we're leaving Hester Street."

"And where are we going? Another shtetl, Sam?"

"I'll talk to Bernstein. We'll make a deal for a partnership and we'll move. You cannot stay here anymore. I'll borrow enough money from Bernstein. Hester Street can no longer be our home. The memories are not good for us anymore."

The family moved to Brooklyn as soon as he and Bernstein could come to an agreement on a partnership deal. The B & B Bedding Company opened for operation a scant six months after the terrible Triangle Shirtwaist fire took the life of Rachel Steiner.

Sam and Eva found several apartments in Brooklyn not too far from the new B & B Bedding Company and moved into one of them. They had more comfort; there was a small room for Mildred's crib.

The memory of the Triangle Shirtwaist Fire began to fade. Hester Street became a very sad memory that Eva could finally recall without crying. Whenever she thought of Rachel Steiner the tears returned for a little while. She and Sam remembered some of the good times they had there. Eve slowly returned to a more relaxed and happier life. She adored Mildred and spent a good deal of her time walking down the wide boulevard they had moved to.

An immense dedication together with a driving desire to be successful in their new country drove the two partners. Hard work, dreadfully long hours, a strong and consistent meeting of their minds together with a careful blending of their talents led them to a slow but steady growth.

B & B Bedding began to build its reputation as a firm of reliable craftsmen who never cut corners. Their products could be counted on to last for years of use. Whenever a flaw was discovered or reported to them, it was either repaired or replaced at no charge to the customer. Sam paid his partner back the money he had borrowed to move.

The calluses on Sam's hands became a protective cushion and he was able to perform his duties better and faster as time went on. He insisted that they purchase the best steel springs on the market and the toughest twine available to insure their product was the best in the market place.

Schlomo Bernstein brought his full weight to bear jumping up and down on every finished box spring before it was shipped to its destination.

"It's got to have the right bounce to it, Bernstein. You have to make sure it does. One drop not enough and we tighten or loosen the cord on the springs until you say it's perfect."

"I'll make sure it bounces, Brandeis, not to worry."

"And, Bernstein, the mattress has to be a perfect fit on top of the springs. A little here and a little there over or under and our reputation goes down the drain. It has to be exact. I think we should keep the front room of the place for our products and our customers only, like a showroom. They should have a place to sit and be comfortable and it should be clean. And when they come in, that's what you tell them and that's what you show them; perfect fit and the bounce that will give them a good night's sleep. A little glass of tea might go good too."

"That's what I always do, Brandeis, make the offer of a glass of tea."

"I didn't mean to tell you how to sell, Bernstein. I know you can sell any customer quicker than anyone I've ever known."

"Why thank you, Brandeis. The first compliment is always appreciated."

"Being your partner is the real compliment, Bernstein. That's first last and always."

The B & B Bedding Co. hired a trucking company to make their deliveries. Schlomo Bernstein was in charge of all their deliveries and he had the final say in who was hired to make their deliveries.

"Brandeis, I think one of us should learn to drive. If and when we can afford it, we can buy a used truck and make our own deliveries. It will save us a fortune."

"Who's going to be this wonderful driver?"

"Brandeis, your eyes are much better than mine. You're younger and stronger than I am. I think it should be you."

Sam thought the idea over many times until their business began to show a steady profit.

"Bernstein, I think you were right. I'll get a license to drive a truck. If business keeps up, we'll get a small truck, one that can carry four or five springs at a time, and I'll make deliveries. If we continue to show a profit, we can hire a man who can help with the deliveries and when he's not in the truck with me, he can sweep up and keep the place clean. It will make a better impression on customers."

Sam learned to drive and they bought a pick-up truck. His first deliveries were an adventure as he didn't know many of the addresses of their customers. He learned Brooklyn slowly and added Manhattan to his knowledge. The Bronx and Queens customers had their mattresses delivered by the trucking company they used for all their out-of-neighborhood deliveries.

One day, while Sam was tinkering in the shop, he came up with several designs and different shapes for sturdy legs to attach to their box springs.

"Bernstein, does our competition put legs on their bedding?"

"Not too much, Brandeis. I haven't seen legs on box springs, yet."

Sam showed Schlomo Bernstein his designs for small legs that fit compactly on the frame underneath the springs. He tried them out on their finished products.

"Works good, Brandeis. Even more solid than before. No shaking on the springs, with or without the mattress. What's the cost?"

"Not so much, Bernstein. The lumber is cheap and I can make all sizes and shapes for the same money. Why don't we begin without charging extra for the legs? It might cut down the profit a little, but I'm willing to bet it increases the sales, especially if no one else has it yet."

"I'm not so sure it's worth the cost, Brandeis, but let's give it a try. I'll add it to our ad on our page in the telephone book for the nest issue."

"We can have a sign printed and put in the window and on the sides of the truck. If we're going to do it, let's do it right."

B & B Bedding continued to show a steady profit. The legs made problems because the shapes were not always to the customer's taste. Sam never said 'no' to any customer and he was soon making legs of every possible shape and design. Schlomo made deals with a tire dealer if they bought all four tires at one time. He was also able to arrange a deal for gas and oil more cheaply. He fought over the price of every repair the truck needed and they were able to hire a man to accompany Sam on deliveries and keep the showroom part of their factory clean and neat. The man also cleaned up the mess that Sam left while he was making their products or experimenting with new ideas.

As B & B succeeded, Sam prospered. Eva gave birth to a child every 18 months and in the period of approximately five years the Brandeis family consisted of four children. Mildred who was born in the shtetl, her two new sisters, Anna, who, when she married was my mother, and Ceilia who were born in Brooklyn,

USA. On her last pregnancy, Eva Brandeis finally gave birth to a son.

"Eva you have given birth four times. Once don't count. It's enough. We have a son now. You should give your body a rest now."

"Me? It's you Sam who doesn't leave me time to rest."

It was the first time in years that Sam had dared to mention the fire and the death of Rachel Steiner and the baby they lost. He looked at his wife for a reaction, some trace that she still suffered from memories of that dreadful night but there was no visible sign on her face that he could see.

"But a son, Eva. I love all the girls and I always will, but a son to carry on the name of Brandeis is special. A son who can own my part of B & B Bedding when the time comes. There is no one in America who has more than I have. I will build him a cradle like you never saw, Eva. It will rock back and forth and it will have bells on it so that it sings whenever Abraham, our son, moves. His name will be Abraham, after your dear father. If you want another name, you can put it between Abraham and Brandeis, that's OK with me. I will tell Schlomo to make a mattress that is so comfortable that Abraham will fall asleep the minute he lays down on it. I will put a pedal on it so if you want to you can rock him without having to bend down. Oh, Eva, wait until you see what I will make for our son."

"You don't think your daughters will be jealous?"

"Jealous? They'll be fighting to see who can take care of him, not who is jealous. Wait and see, Eva, wait and you'll see."

"They'll be jealous Sam that you made a cradle for him and not for them."

"Eva, if I have to I will make a small cradle for each of them so they can put their dolls in it, just like you put their brother in his. There will be no jealousy between our children, not in this house. There is no room for that."

Mrs. Bernstein was not able to have children and adoption was out of the question for Schlomo. Instead they took over various roles with the Brandeis' children and became 'Aunt Blanche' and 'Uncle Schlomo'.

"Eva, it is time that we do not celebrate Passover without the Bernstein's at our table. They belong with us and our children who love them dearly. No more Passovers without the Bernstein's.

The Passover Seder was a joy to behold; Eva and Blanche cooked for several days before; there was enough food so that many neighbors were invited for the festival. The lighting of the Chanukah lights gave birth to a similar celebration for the two partners and their neighbors except this went on for eight nights with a different gathering for each night of the holiday.

"Bernstein, I'm thinking of a larger home for the Brandeis family. It is getting crowded and Eva thinks it would be good if each child could have his or her own room."

"You're talking a mansion, Sam, not a home. You've got a lot of children."

"I know, but if the two girls Mildred and Ceilia sleep together in the largest bedroom, in their own beds of course, and Abie and Anna each have their own room with their own beds, we could make it easily. We would only need three bedrooms that way."

"And a cafeteria to eat in."

"I think we could manage. I'm talking to you, Schlomo, because I know you're thinking of buying a car, even though you tell me how blind you've gotten. If you do buy a car, which I think you should, then I could drive the truck home after the last delivery at night and bring it back in the morning."

"That's an idea, Brandeis."

"I mention it in that way, Bernstein, because if that could be worked out, Eva and I could move a little bit further away from the store where we are now, without adding time for traveling to and from the store. We could maybe even afford to buy a small house. If the traveling to and from the store were not a problem anymore, I could let my thoughts think in a different direction."

"Let them go, Brandeis. What's good for your family is what you should think of. If you want to take the truck home, take it. Don't let moving a little further away from the plant get in the way of your plans. And don't wait for me and Blanche to buy a car. We'll get one when we're ready for one. Let your thoughts and Eva's thoughts go wherever they want to go. Plan to do you and the family the most good."

"Did you ever wonder, Bernstein, why I call it a store or a place and you call it a plant?"

"If I wondered such a thing, I don't remember it, Brandeis. What's the difference if we're both talking about the plant where we're making such a good living?"

"I don't know Bernstein. I just wondered."

"If that's what you do when you're driving the truck all over or driving nails into the frames, you'd better take a long vacation, Brandeis."

"Some day, Bernstein, a vacation will be in order, one for each of us."

"We'll have to work that out Brandeis, sooner rather than later."

After months of slowly building their reputation, a paled-face Schlomo Bernstein confronted his partner after one of their most difficult days in the store. Everything seemed to have gone wrong.

"Sam, we've got to have conversation."

"Conversation? We're not talking anymore, Bernstein, we're conversing?"

"We need to talk, Sam."

"So we'll talk, Bernstein."

The partners were standing in front of the part of the store they called "the showroom", checking on a delivery of merchandise from a new supplier.

"Close the front door, Sam and we'll go in the back office. I don't want our conversation to be interrupted."

"Sounds serious, Bernstein, since I just became "Sam" instead of "Brandeis". We've been using last names since day one and now I'm "Sam" instead of Brandeis. It must be serious, Bernstein."

"It's serious; Okay, Brandeis if you prefer. Unfortunately it is very serious."

"Two names instead of one. That's real serious. I hope it's not Blanche, Bernstein. She didn't take a turn for the worse?"

"No, Brandeis, it's not Blanche. It's me."

"You? What's wrong with you, Bernstein?"

Schlomo Bernstein turned the sign on the front door from "OPEN" to "CLOSED".

"Let's go in the back office, Brandeis."

"I'm Brandeis again?"

"It's no time for jokes, Sam. C'mon into the back office."

Sam followed his partner to the back office. As they walked, Sam saw that Schlomo Bernstein's shoulders were badly slumped making him look, from behind, years older, an old man he didn't recognize. He took a seat at the desk opposite Schlomo.

"So, Bernstein, we're talking. What is it with you? Are you sick?"

"In a way, Brandeis, in a way, I'm really sick."

When he looked more closely at his partner, he saw that Schlomo Bernstein's face had turned to an eerie-looking gray color. He knew for a week or two Schlomo hadn't been looking well, but he surmised that it was his wife Blanche who must have had bad news from her doctor.

"I didn't mention it, Bernstein, but lately you haven't been looking like yourself. Naturally I assumed it was bad news about Blanche."

"Sam, all that stuff I told you about Blanche was a lie, an out and out lie, among many other lies. She's as healthy as a horse and will outlive us all. I asked you not to talk about it front in of her so my real problem would not become part of the conversation. I didn't want her or you to know what's going on with me."

"So, what's going on with you, Bernstein?"

Sam Brandeis was having difficulty believing the words coming out of Schlomo Bernstein. He stared at his partner in disbelief.

"Bernstein, I'm a lousy guesser and a worse speculator. Talk to me; what is it? What's going on with you?"

"Listen to me, Brandeis. I'm the one with the disease. It's called gambling. It's a real demon and it kills faster than cancer. I bet on the horses, Sam, every day. Twice a week, I go to a secret place and play poker in a high-stakes game where I can't afford to lose."

"My God, Bernstein, this is all news to me. I had no idea."

"Of course you didn't, Sam. I wouldn't dare tell you or anyone else. I'm in this mess all by my stupid self. Even the new car I bought is mixed up with me in this mess."

"How bad is it, Bernstein? If it's money, how much are we talking about?"

"I can't stop, Brandeis. I keep trying to get even with the bastards, but every day, every night I get in deeper. It's got a strangle-hold on my throat. I can't breathe. It's already no use. I just can't stop, Brandeis."

"That's why I'm all of a sudden "Sam" and then "Brandeis"? Changing my name won't help. You're telling me now because you owe more than you can pay?"

"It's worse than that, Sam. I'm into the sharks for thousands. I'm up to the point where they're not willing to wait any more. They say they're tired of my excuses. The threats are getting worse. If they thought for one minute that killing me would get them their money, I'd be dead."

"A number, Bernstein, give me a number so I'll know what-in-hell we're talking about."

"Brandeis, you haven't got that much cash, believe me. I can't even say that number out loud. I choke on it, thinking about it."

"Bernstein, stop the crap. Say the damned number out loud, NOW. If you're going to choke, so choke."

Sam Brandeis looked at the shell of the man seated opposite him; a person he thought he knew as well as any other person he had ever known, including Luca Steiner and even his wife, Eva. Tears were rolling down Schlomo Bernstein's gray cheeks. Sam realized that the bones of his face had become more sharply etched. He began to sob. Strange noises were coming from deep within his body. He buried his head in his hands and slumped on the desk. Sam saw a man in front of him he had never seen before.

"I can assume Blanche doesn't have any idea about this?"

"Assume, Sam, assume anything you want. They took the car away from me two weeks ago. A 'partial' the bastards called it. A 'partial'. I told Blanche it was in the shop getting a repair it needed. I had to tell her some of the truth when she threatened to go to you. She's a 'partial'. My life is now a 'partial', Brandeis."

"She knows the whole story?"

"She's knows only a 'partial'. I told her I had an accident. She knows only what I told her and I told her as little as I could. Blanche is a 'partial', also. She thought the car was still in the shop. She had a visitor yesterday. A big, black guy, so big he couldn't even fit through the door of the apartment without ducking. He threatened her and told her how much money she owes. Not me alone, but her also. We both owe it he told her. Me and her. He said they would take it out of her ass after they got it out of mine."

"Bernstein, good God, give me a number. Talk to me. We'll work something out if I know what-in-hell we're talking about. A number, Bernstein, a number."

"It's more than $25,000, Brandeis."

Another dreadful noise came out of Schlomo Bernstein. Sam thought it wasn't even a human sound.

"Is there any more, Bernstein? Really, the whole thing, Bernstein, the real dollars we have to deal with."

"About 10 G's more, Sam. Maybe closer to 15 G's more Sam with the "vig". The total is about 40,000 Sam."

Sam Brandeis sat quietly across from the sobbing figure of his partner, trying to contemplate a four followed by four more zeros.

"I can go to the bank, Bernstein. I'll get a loan on my share of the business. It's worth more than that."

"I already went to the bank, Brandeis. The only

collateral they would accept is the business. I couldn't do that; I wouldn't do that to you and anyway, they needed both signatures or they wouldn't even talk to me. I couldn't find the nerve to tell you, Brandeis that you have a sick, thieving partner. That's when I gave the bastards the car. If B & B Bedding has any collateral value, I already used it all up. The men at the bank know I'm in financial trouble, Sam."

"Mr. Palermo, the President of the bank will make an arrangement with me."

"He won't Brandeis, I know it. If I have money trouble, he knows you do too. And he knows that what I have is a disease, a real disease and he won't take a chance or lend money on that kind of sickness. He as much told me so."

"You've got to stop this insanity, Bernstein. No more gambling."

"Brandeis, you didn't listen. You didn't hear a word I said. It's a sickness, a terrible sickness. I can't stop it, I can't. It doesn't go away by itself. It's like a cancer, but there's no cure for it, no injections. And the bastards won't wait anymore. We've got to protect you and your family's interests. We got to go back to the lawyer who made out all the papers in the beginning and get him to change everything. He's got to get me out of the business and get it all in your name. I must disappear to protect you and Eva. He'll know how to do it and I'll sign any papers I have to so I can separate me from you. I wouldn't wait another day, not even an hour. We'll go to the lawyer tomorrow, Brandeis."

"Now I understand how I became "Sam", instead of Brandeis. You've called me Brandeis since the day we met. Now you're writing me off because you're in trouble. What kind of partner do you think I am? Trouble is trouble for both of us."

"You want to be Brandeis, be Brandeis. I don't know what I'm saying or doing anymore. Names don't mean anything, Brandeis. We've got to take actions at once to protect the business from those bastards, those vultures, and from me."

There was a pounding on the front door.

"Don't answer; don't go Brandeis, it might be them. They might do you harm. Sam, sit here; don't go."

Sam got up from behind the desk and walked slowly to the front door. He turned and looked at his partner. The teary gray face did not resemble any face he had ever seen. He continued walking through the showroom to the front door. He could see Blanche Bernstein through the glass of the front door standing outside, pounding on it with her fists. Sam ran to the door and let her in. She grabbed Sam and stood in the vestibule. She started to cry. Her perfume clogged his nostrils and he had to step back from her.

"Oh, Sam, you don't know, you don't know."

"I know Blanche, I know. Schlomo just told me. C'mon inside instead of standing outside. He's in the office, in the back."

"I don't want to see him Sam. He's ruined all of us and he'll ruin Eva and you, too. I don't want to see him, ever again, Sam. There were strangers ringing my bell all day long. Big men, scary men, ugly men. They told me Schlomo owes them thousands and I owe them thousands too. They told me they'd get it any way they could, even if it had to come out of my backside."

"He's got a sickness, Blanche. Sick people have to be cared for and made well by those who care for them."

"Did he care about me when he did what he did? I'm not going home, Sam, now or ever. I'll find a hotel where nobody knows me. I'll let you know where I am if I get there safely with my ass in one piece. I trust you and only you. No one else knows except you and me and that stupid rat I married. He's been lying to me so much I'll never believe him again. Don't tell him I was here Sam, please don't. I'll call you when I know where I'll be. Goodbye."

Blanche Bernstein stifled a cry and ran out into the street. She turned once to look at Sam. He watched Blanche as she crossed the street and turned at the first corner she came to. He watched until he was sure no one had followed her. He closed the door and made his way back to the office where Schlomo Bernstein sat sobbing, his head shaking between his hands.

They went back to the attorney who had done the original work on the B & B Bedding Co. He listened to their sad, sad story, shaking his head back and forth, almost in rhythm to the way Sam and Schlomo were relating what had happened.

"Unfortunately, I've heard this song before. Oy, gambling my friends, there is no sure way out of the hole you have gotten yourselves into. I can't be responsible for what gangsters are capable of and how hard they'll push you to get their dirty *gelt* from you. I will dissolve B & B immediately after you leave the office. There will be papers to sign, which I'll have prepared for you both by late tomorrow afternoon when you return. Both of you must be here at five sharp. Legally, I will protect you both from them; physically, I make no promises. *Mamzers,* (bastards) come in all shapes and sizes, and every degree of nasty you could dream of. They're not anyone's 'cup of tea'."

The lawyer sat and looked at the men who had come to him for help.

"I'll need a new name. B & B must disappear from the world as we know it.

Will The Manor Bedding Corp. do?"

"What about the police? Is there no help from them?"

"Sam, the answer is no, not really. There is protection, but Schlomo will have to tell them where he gambles, provide at least addresses and names if he can. Your friends in the gambling business know that as well as I do, and usually, they act faster than the cops can. And, there are more of them than there are cops, in any neighborhood. Disappearance is a strange concept, Schlomo, but after we get the papers together and signed, that's what I would recommend. Take Blanche and the both of you disappear. For how long or even where, I have no advice. I don't want to know. I wouldn't stay here or take chances for any length of time."

"Any name you pick is good. Manor Bedding is OK with me."

"You don't count anymore, Schlomo. Sam?"

"Manor, 'Schmanor'. I don't care."

"I'll take care of it quickly. As I said, be here tomorrow at 5 PM sharp. I'll be waiting for you and be careful. Come here without any escorts."

Sam went to the synagogue every day to pray for Schlomo. He wasn't sure exactly what he was praying for, but he knew his partner was in desperate straits and needed some kind of shoulder to lean on. If it had to be prayer in the synagogue he would give it to Schlomo; if it had to be a prayer to God in any form, Sam would give that to him. Sam would give nourishment to Schlomo in any way he could, no questions asked. Sam swore an oath that whatever he could "*shlep*" from the bank, he would give to Schlomo.

"You're going to throw good money after bad, you fool? I wouldn't be partners with anyone who would even suggest such a stupid thing, Sam Brandeis. Take my advice and your money, shut up and run from me. Not another word."

A week later, B & B Bedding was dissolved. All business associations, and any traces of Sam and Schlomo's partnership had been removed. Signed, sealed and delivered, there was no longer a Bernstein in the bedding business. Sam Brandeis was the sole owner and proprietor of the Manor Bedding Corp.

Privately, Sam made a stipulation with the lawyer: Blanche Bernstein was to receive whatever share her husband would have received if there had been a legal sale and a settlement for B & B Bedding.

"You don't have to do this, Brandeis. He brought this on himself."

"Mrs. Bernstein has to live. She didn't do anything wrong. We'll have to figure out a way so those bastards won't bother her. You do that, and please and give me the bill."

At the end of the following month, Sam found out that Schlomo had disappeared. Blanche called him long distance, told him there was no trace of her husband, thanked him for the arrangement he had made and hung up before he could find out where she was. Weeks later, there was a two line notice in a New York paper that Schlomo Bernstein had been found dead, an apparent suicide.

chapter 6

My Story

IT WAS HARD FOR ME to believe that one year to the day had passed since Sam Brandeis had died. The invitation to the cemetery appeared in my mail box, even though the date and time of the actual event were burned into my memory.

I was at the cemetery once again, this time for the celebration of Sam's soul rising to heaven in accordance with Jewish traditional law. The ritual was called by the God-awful name, *"the unveiling",* which the entire family along with treasured old friends was gathered at Sam's grave for this particular day's celebration.

My automobile and I studiously tried to avoid the dour woman I had grown to dislike so quickly a year ago. It was evidently part of her job on this particular day to direct traffic. She stood outside her office daring anyone to pass her without being instructed to the site where the ceremony was to be held. However much I didn't want to see her again and be lectured on whatever her subject was for the day, she was blocking my path to Sam's grave. I was pretty certain that Sam's children, my mother, her two sisters and her brother, my uncle, had made all the proper arrangements for this day. If a Rabbi was needed he would be in attendance with an ample supply of stones.

The woman recognized either me or the car I was driving as she seemed to snort aloud. She forced me to put on the brakes and come to a complete stop. I rolled down the window.

"I'm glad to know that there are some in your family who know what the correct thing to do in a cemetery is, young man."

Her smell was as strong as her words.

"Yes, Ma'am, there are those who know. I hope they have the correct amount of stones."

She snorted and turned away from me. It was just in time. I rolled up the window as quickly as I could as I feared her odor would pervade the car for the rest of the day.

Sam's three daughters were all married and the second, Anna, as previously noted, my mother, was there with my father, Max and my sister. I had come alone as I figured I had attained an age where I could be trusted to come to the right place at the right time and not get killed or re-routed. My Aunt Mildred and her husband Bob were in attendance along with my Aunt Celia and her husband, Max. When my sister saw me drive up, she came to my car and she clung onto my arm from the moment she saw me exit from my car.

"I wasn't sure you would be here, Richard," she said, happy to see that I had arrived safely and on time. Her memories of any truculent behavior I had exhibited during the years we had grown up together hadn't been disturbed by the passage of some adult years.

"You must have been listening too closely to either your mother or your father or both."

My favorite Uncle, Sam's son Abe, had married unusually late in life because he felt a deep love and responsibility for both his parents. He had difficulty finding a woman who was able to appreciate his commitment and sincere love for them. When he did find Beatrice, he married her, about a year ago. The abiding obligation he carried for them remained deep within his heart. She was pregnant and had stayed at home for this day in charge of the preparations for the house-full of guests that were expected there after the service.

My sister and I were the only grandchildren of Sam Brandeis' who were there. All the excuses I heard seemed to add up to distances that were too far and or too expensive or both. Mildred and Bob had moved to Philadelphia, as he was pursuing his career goals in merchandising. They saw no need for their only child to come to Queens for this particular event. Celia and Max were living in California for the past seven years and they also saw no urgency for their children to take up two expensive seats on an airplane for someone they hardly knew. The short supply of close family relatives made the gathering of Sam's friends from the business world and the members of his synagogue that had known him and coveted him in life and death seem three or four time larger in comparison to the family members that had taken the time to honor Sam Brandeis' memory on that day.

After I greeted those who I knew, I found the Rabbi who was to conduct the service. Sam had proudly introduced me to him when I visited the synagogue during a service on a Saturday morning. I had spoken to him every time I had visited the synagogue where Sam worshipped. I had drawn him into my confidence a year ago and he helped me to make sure that Sam Brandeis had been buried with the box he treasured so much. I bluntly asked him if he thought the box which he put next to Sam, was still inside the coffin.

"Of course it is, Richard. It was his dying wish. He wanted it, you wanted it and I made it happened. I'm sure it's still with him."

"Thank you, Rabbi. One more question. That woman, standing there alone, do you know her?"

Rabbi Hirsh looked to where I was pointing.

"I don't exactly know her, Richard. I do know that she was once a part of Sam's past that he didn't want to talk about."

"Talk about a surprise, Rabbi. I never heard of her or saw her before today."

"She was in Sam's life, long before you were born. I would guess that no one in your family knows about her either."

"But you do, Rabbi. I can hear it in your voice."

"I only know what Sam told me. He knew her once probably long ago. He was reluctant to mention any more to me than that."

"Wow, Rabbi. That's news to me. No one ever mentioned another woman in Sam's life to me."

"She wasn't 'another woman' in any sense, Richard. Probably no one in your family ever heard of her, either. She was probably the wife of Sam's former partner, Schlomo Bernstein. They were in business together. Their firm was called the B & B Bedding Co. They used to refer to it jokingly as "the three B's; not Bach, not Beethoven, not Brahms, but Bedding, Bernstein and Brandeis". Sam told me they were successful until Mr. Bernstein succumbed to a dreadful gambling habit that strangled him and almost bankrupted the firm."

"Wow, Rabbi, I never heard of anything like that."

"As I said, Sam was reticent about speaking of him or her or their business."

"Do you know what happened to that Mr. Bernstein and their business?"

"Mr. Bernstein and their business were evidently being threatened by mobsters that he owed a fortune to. Sam told me that upon Mr. Bernstein's advice and a lawyer's advice, they dissolved the firm immediately, split up their partnership and went their separate ways. After all the arrangements were completed, Sam went into business again, this time as the Manor Bedding Corp. without any partners."

I looked at the woman again. She stared back at me.

"I'm sure no one in the family is aware of any of that, Rabbi."

"Probably not, Richard. You grandmother, maybe. As you must realize, none of them was alive at the time. The woman in black over there left Mr. Bernstein, out of fear of the mobsters or just plain anger over what her husband had done. A few months later, Mr. Bernstein was reported as a suicide. That was when your grandfather came to talk to me. He told me the whole story and asked my advice as to how he should treat his former partner's wife, Mrs. Bernstein.

"We spoke for a long time, Sam and I. I'm not completely sure of the results of our conversation, but I believe he made some kind of settlement with her so she wouldn't be destitute at the time they split up their partnership."

'Speechlessness' was not part of my nature, but the Rabbi's story did it. I couldn't say anything.

"I know you can understand that Sam didn't speak about this episode. I have no idea what he told your grandmother, or if he told her anything. I never asked him and he never mentioned the affair to me again, Richard."

"That's quite a story, Rabbi Hirsh, quite a story."

"It is my belief that you should keep all this to yourself. I can see nothing that would be gained by speaking of this to anyone, Richard. There are times when 'letting sleeping dogs lie' is good, solid advice."

"Rabbi, do you think I should go and speak to the woman?"

"Absolutely not. I can see no reason for you to speak to her or even try to. That would generate more questions that no one alive now could answer."

"Sounds like advice I better follow, Rabbi."

"At Sam's home later on, Richard, there will be questions about what the two of us were talking about. You can tell them that I was double checking on some of the things I wanted to say about Sam in my eulogy. You can mention that there were names I wanted to include without leaving out anyone that was important to Sam."

"That sounds like something I can do, easily, Rabbi.

Whatever 'sleeping dogs' there may have been in Sam's life shall remain fast asleep."

I turned for one last look at the woman. She was grinding a cigarette under her heel. She looked at me, then at the grave and then she hurried away.

Rabbi Hirsh called the visitors together; they made a closed circle around the gravesite. He waited for absolute quiet. He said a few prayers in Hebrew and then continued in English. His tribute to the man I treasured so much during his life span on earth was measured. His words contained sentiments and feelings that were not the usual accolades from ceremonies such as this one. He was not reading from a short biography arranged for by close relations that so many Rabbis concocted for times like this. He spoke as lovingly about Sam Brandeis as I would have and he meant every word he said. I would tell him so before the day was over. The ceremony ended. Some mourners left rocks on the gravestone. I knew I would leave two rocks; one for the woman in black and one for…me?

It was a cloudless sky; the tears in my eyes burned from the sun above. Maybe Sam thought these things were as superfluous as I did, but the keeping of tradition was enough to make it strategically important for him as well as for millions of other followers and believers of the religion. My belief that it was far more a consolation for the living had no bearing on what Sam thought during his lifetime. It must be noted, however, that whatever my belief was, I did look for the cloud in the sky that might have hidden Sam from my view.

I looked up at the sky several times before I got back into my car. I sat quietly, reflecting on the man I loved so much for so many years. A cloud began to cover the sun. The day grew a shade darker. I hesitated. I looked up into the sky one more time. I saw his face, smiling his beautiful smile. I could see his blue eyes twinkling as brightly as ever.

"A mitzvah, Pitchela Ritchela, a mitzvah. I have my box beside me."

The cloud passed. His smile seemed brighter as I drove out of the cemetery. I was on the Inter-Boro Parkway again protecting myself from the vagaries of its designer. Driving back to Sam's home, I tried to reconstruct everything Rabbi Hirsh had told me. It was stunning for me to realize that there were parts of Sam's life that were filled with drama, great successes and even some failures, that I knew nothing about and never even heard of. I couldn't help but wonder how much more there might be that was unknown to me.

I assumed that my parents and my other relatives had tried to ascertain who the woman in black was with absolutely no success. I had agreed with the Rabbi that if I were asked about her, my answer would be that I didn't know who she was and that I had never seen her before, period. That part was the plain, unvarnished truth.

By the time I reached my destination, there was no place to park my car within several blocks of Sam's home. I wasn't in any hurry so I drove around until I found a satisfactory place to leave my automobile. I walked slowly back to Coney Island Avenue.

When I turned the corner there were several people entering Sam's home. They seemed like the tail end of a congratulatory line at the conclusion of a wedding waiting to greet the bride or the groom or both. I later realized that I was looking for the woman in black. She wasn't anywhere to be seen, of course.

I expected that there would be more tears from the immediate family, but all the women were in the kitchen preparing various foods to eat and soft drinks for every taste. I also knew there would be memories that included Sam Brandeis in a starring role. I hoped that the sadness, so much in evidence at the gravesite, would have been eased for a great many of the mourners. I appreciated that the appetites that had been held off for several hours was on many minds as well as the deep sadness that brought them to this house.

I found my Uncle Abe and told him I needed a drink.

"You driving?"

"Yes, I am."

"Don't overdo. You know where it is. It's not hidden from you. If anyone asks, it's medicine."

"Truer words were never spoken. Medicine it is, especially today. Will you join me?"

"Not for that stuff. How you can drink scotch is beyond me."

"Blame it on your sister. She taught me."

"Anna is one good drinker."

"All her life. I think she's built a wall around herself so she's always under control, even on a day like today. I know she's sad about gram'pa too, but if you didn't know her, you'd never believe it. Private Channa, gram'pa used to call her."

"I didn't know that."

"Well, now you do. Private Channa, like she was in the Army."

"I'm sure there will be stories from those inside that will sound like "David and Goliath" with all of them playing the part of "David", I said.

"That's okay. Gram'pa never needed to assume the role of a "David". He knew who he was all the time. Never a doubt in him."

"Before you go back inside, Uncle Abe, did you know that gram'pa had a partner once?"

"I think I remember hearing Ma mentioning it once or twice. It didn't seem to matter to her and Papa never mentioned it, so I never asked about it. Why do you ask?"

"Rabbi Hirsh said something about it to me about it. The rabbi wanted to make sure that he didn't have to mention it in his eulogy if it wasn't important to Sam or any visitors, today."

"I wonder why he asked you."

"I think I was just "handy" at the moment he brought it up. I think that's all there was too it."

"You're probably right. I'm going back to the living room. Finish your 'medicine' and c'mon inside."

I was pretty sure that my memories of my grandfather would be interesting to many of the people who knew him well, back in the old days. It occurred to me that I might hear from any one of them more about that part of his life that I had no knowledge of. Some of them went much further back than I did. I finished my drink and went back into the living room. Irving Stark, a man who had done business with Sam long ago, was holding forth.

"In business, Brandeis was a fair customer, but a very difficult retailer. His strongest bargaining argument was: take 'im' or 'leave 'im'. I'm sure most of you who did business with him heard it more than once. I remember him quoting a price to me and walking around the merchandise in question and then daring me to find anything better anywhere in the world.

When I questioned him on that score, he said: 'take 'im' or leave 'im'. When Brandeis reached that sentiment, it was all over, end of discussion. He really was ready to put his merchandise back on the truck that brought it. Tough in business, but reasonably fair."

"You're so right, Irv," chimed in Joe Monroe. "I remember clearly that once I tried to get him to go along with not charging me sales tax on one of his invoices. It happened to be the largest order I had ever placed with him. I didn't see any harm in asking him to do me that little favor. It would have saved me a bundle. Sam looked me in the eye, said the same phrase you're talking about and then asked me if I was some kind of Nazi or something. I decided he had to be kidding, so I asked him if he was Uncle Sam. Mistake, mistake, Mistake."

Joe Monroe waited until the laughter died down.

"Your Uncle? Never, *you goniff*", (thief) he yelled at me. "If I had to, I would change my name to *alter cocker* before I would be your uncle. Uncle Sam is a nickname for *my* country. I don't cheat on my country. Uncle Sam invited me to live here, to become a citizen here and you're asking me to cheat on him? Of course you all know the phrase that followed that."

A chorus of voices rang out: "take 'im' or leave 'im' followed by more good natured laughter. I listened to more stories about Sam from the assembled crowd.

"Take 'im' or leave 'im' seemed to be the most popular expression that most remembered Sam repeating. My Uncle Abe finally spoke up.

"My father only used that expression during the war. I had an exemption from the Army because I was the sole support of my parents. For the first two years of the war, I spent every dollar I made buying up every steel spring I could. I made more box springs than I could count because I knew my exemption couldn't last. The springs were stored in the garage. When my exemption was over and I finally was called to serve in the Army, I had left my father a garage full of box springs so he could make some kind of living more than the twenty-one dollars a month they were paying me, which I sent back to him. He used 'take 'im' or leave 'im' because he was selling what he called "my Abie's" labor, and to cut even a nickel from his price would be a betrayal and somehow sacrilegious to him because it would be taking away what I had worked for and left for him and my mother. I was defending our country and he was defending my labor. He wouldn't have been able to live with himself if he sold any of those box springs for a penny under the price he thought was fair and right."

There was a decided lull in the conversation after my Uncle Abe had given his explanation of take 'im' or leave 'im'. I thought he might have asked if anyone there knew Sam had a partner. He didn't. I looked at Rabbi Hirsh who was still in the room and he nodded to me in relief as he knew that I was thinking exactly what he was thinking.

I sat silently in the room, sipping my Johnnie Walker and listening to more stories about Sam Brandeis, the way he did business and other memories that others in the room were willing to share. 'Take 'im or leave 'im' seemed to have made an indelible impression on most of those who were willing to talk about Sam. There were many stories and encounters I had never heard about and several others I had heard it repeated various times when Sam was in a mood to share memories with an audience of friends.

Abe's wife, Beatrice came into the room with a tray filled with more delicacies. Her pregnancy kept her home to supervise the preparations to make sure everything went smoothly when everyone returned from the cemetery. She stood quietly holding the tray in front of each guest, urging them to take something to eat.

"Don't be bashful," she said to anyone that hesitated. "If you don't eat, Sam will be displeased. Knowing him, he might come back to haunt us all."

"Take 'im' or leave 'im'" I said to a room that suddenly burst into laughter once again.

Beatrice waited until the tray was emptied. She left

and I followed her into the kitchen. I thought I would be more comfortable there and that's where the scotch was.

The kitchen was still a beehive of feminine activity. Trays were washed and dried and then piled high with freshly made food. Any suggestion of using paper plates had been vetoed two days before by Beatrice and Sam's daughters.

I found the Johnnie Walker Black and had another drink. The women were still talking about the strange woman who stood behind a tree. Their questions seemed to hang in the air, going unanswered. They decided that if no one came forward with an explanation of who the woman was, it would remain a mystery forever.

"Maybe Sam once sold her a box spring and she read about the unveiling somewhere and she decided to come. Why don't you leave it at that?"

I went back into the living room and sat down.

"Brandeis always spoke about you as if he thought you were someone special," Leon Greene said to me.

"My Grandfather was the special one in the family. I was only special because I was the first male child born in the family. I think he would have felt that way about the first born male whoever he was."

My mother appeared with another tray piled high.

"Anyone that knew my father well had to know that he did prefer males. You can check with any of his daughters who are in the kitchen and they'll tell you the same thing. Sam Brandeis preferred males."

"C'mon, Mom, he wasn't that prejudiced."

"You Grandfather had his favorites and he had no problem expressing them."

"As we all do, Mom."

My mother left the room when her tray had been emptied.

Leon Greene came and sat down next to me.

"You go back further than most of us who did business with Sam."

"Family usually does."

"So, *boychik*, first arrival or what, it's your turn to talk about the Sam Brandeis you knew. We all knew him one way. You knew a different Sam Brandeis. You knew the inner man, so to speak."

"Listen to Greene. A philosopher, yet."

"If it sounds like I'm bragging," I said, "it's because I am. I think Sam Brandeis was a genius in many ways. For instance, I can remember my father bringing his ten-year old Studebaker here to Sam because it huffed and puffed and died."

"It didn't die, Richard," my father interrupted me. "It stalled."

"Whatever it did, it did it. I remember Sam told my father to turn her on."

My father turned the engine on again. It huffed and it puffed and, contrary to other opinions, it died."

"Stalled, Richard," I was corrected again.

"OK, stalled. It didn't matter because while it was running, Sam was listening to it.

"Okay, Max, turn her off."

He opened the hood and peered inside. He looked from the front and from the side and then back to the front again.

"Okay, Max, turn her on one more time, this time with the hood open."

Sam stood back as the engine was started. Same procedure.

"Turn her off, Max."

Sam's both hands went under the hood. They emerged with a dirty part that was dripping with oil and sludge. He went into the shop and came back a few minutes later with the part cleaned and several weird looking screws in one hand. Sam went under the hood again, this time with a rag. He cleaned something inside and screwed the part he had cleaned onto the motor.

"Try her again, Max."

My father turned the motor on; no sputtering, no huffing, no puffing, no stalling and no dying.

"Let her run, Max. I'll go clean up and we'll see."

We had a cup of tea and the motor was still going quietly.

"Turn her off, Max, count to ten and start her up again."

Everything worked the way it was supposed to.

"Take her home again, Max. She's pretty good, almost like new."

My father corroborated the details this time without any comments.

"Any car, any motor, any time he listened and then proceeded, he was able to do something and the broken machine would work again."

One more sip of my drink allowed me to continue.

"I came into his kitchen, one day and he was sitting at the kitchen table with hundreds of parts of their dining room clock spread all over the place."

"She rings wrong, *Richela*. She sounds three rings and she stops. It's no good if she rings three times and it's two o'clock. Don't touch the table. When it's nine o'clock, she stops after three rings. She shouldn't stop. I'll put her back together when I find out what's going on inside her."

"Maybe she's got a belly-ache, Gram'pa."

"If she had a belly-ache, I'd give her to Eva for a 'Bromo'. Everything Eva thinks is broken can be fixed with a 'Bromo'. This is more serious. She doesn't need bubbles, she needs to tighten a screw or put a drop of oil in the right place."

"A look or a listen or both served as his book of instructions," I said.

"Within half-an-hour, every part of the clock was back in its place. It rang correctly on the hour and the half-hour as well. My memory tells me that it had never rung on the half hour before Sam decided 'she needs a look inside'."

"Listen," he said to me. "I turn the hands to one o'clock, she rings once. I turn the hands to nine o'clock, she rings nine times. She's okay, now, without even a 'Bromo'."

He laughed, completely satisfied with himself.

My recitation of Sam's mechanical prowess was followed by several more stories from those present of his ability with machines and anything else that had more than one moving part.

"I remember, everything that had moving parts was a 'she' to Sam", Leon Greene said.

"You're so right. I once asked him about that and he told me one of the foundations of his beliefs.

"If a man breaks, he stays broken; he can't be fixed", he said. "It's over for him. A woman doesn't break so she can always be fixed. So, my grandson, what I can fix is always a "she". That's just the way it is."

Laughter followed my analysis. Irrelevant questions over, for now.

Rabbi Hirsh took over the saga at that point.

"Of course those of you who pray in the same synagogue as Sam knew he actually built a house in back of the synagogue so the congregation could pray outside their synagogue in celebration of their flight from the Egyptian Pharaoh. Jews were supposed to pray away from their synagogue. The holiday is called Succoth and other synagogues have to erect a tent arrangement so as to follow the dictates of that holiday. Sam actually built a house for the congregation that they could use for the length of the holiday."

"I remember that house. It was a marvel for the synagogue, running water, too. No one else had anything like it that I ever heard of," Bernie Greenberg said.

"I was President of the Men's Club at that time," he continued. "The synagogue Men's Club gave him a gold watch the first time they used the house for the holiday. Sam was more proud of that watch than anything I know of. I don't know if any of you can remember, but when Sam was praying in the synagogue, he was always seated in an aisle seat on the right of the synagogue, so the hand with the gold watch could be seen by anyone who passed him walking down the aisle. He would pull his tallis back from his sleeve and pull that sleeve up as high as it would go so that the watch was clearly visible."

"You helped him build that house, didn't you, Richard?"

"Help is a funny word when you're talking about

Sam Brandeis. He "let" me hold some slats straight so he could nail them in properly. I had nails in every pocket and sometimes even in my mouth so I had them ready when he yelled for them. I was able to be of more help with the wiring because I understood electricity. Not better than he did, of course, but Sam had learned to trust me so that he was sure I wouldn't electrocute the two of us. I was the chief of the errand runners. Sam didn't like to leave what he was doing if he could get anyone else to get him what he needed. Looking back now, I know he wanted to build the whole house himself. I don't think he was testing himself, because now I'm sure he could have done it all without any help. I think he wanted to give me a little pride in my abilities and to learn from him the things that weren't in any book he ever heard of."

"*Richela*, if you know you can do it don't let anyone or anything stop you. Do it because you know you can do it, whatever it is."

Others told stories of Sam's prowess with machinery. I decided I would keep for myself the things he did for me personally. He built me a sled and a bicycle; both had Sam's versions of brakes all made from spare parts. He made me a rubber-band gun from polished lumber that could shoot straight farther than the ones the other kids had made from orange crates. He also made what he called a machine gunner that could shoot five pieces of cardboard at one time. When he heard that some mothers complained to mine that it was unfair to their sons that I had so much better 'equipment' his smile was as wide as the Brooklyn Bridge.

The time went more slowly when the memories being related had little or no meaning or made no sense to the listeners; time went more quickly sometimes when it was new to the listeners and had an excitement to it brought by the pulse in the teller's voice. The day began to wear on. People began to leave. Relatives generally stayed the longest.

Many unhappy memories crossed my mind often during the day; a day with tears and kaleidoscopic memories.

chapter 7

Segue

THE YEARS PASSED; SAM BRANDEIS' daughters had married, were raising families of their own and each lived in Brooklyn within walking distance of the Manor Bedding Corp. on Coney Island Avenue. Sam and Eva rented an apartment across the street from the store. Sam bought the building the store was housed in, kept a showroom in the front, added a small room in the back for special projects and kept the two rooms in the back for all the manufacturing activities. He prospered slowly due to the continued quality of his work and his reliability. In the process, he taught his son Abe everything he knew and insisted that Abe was to use absolutely no short cuts in the production of their products.

In his spare time, Sam built an entire apartment above the store. It had originally been used for storage. It was a rat's haven and a menace to anyone who entered it. He hired a huge truck and several men. He cleared the entire slum of the rats, the vermin, the pigeons and other flying things. Sam put in flooring and restored the ceiling below it. Then he built two bedrooms, a full bathroom, a kitchen, a dining room and an extra room in the front so he could sit in his rocking chair and see the world as it went by. The only item he couldn't build was an escalator to take him and Eva upstairs from the store to their living quarters. His children got together; after several hot discussions and accusations as to who could afford what and how much, they presented their parents with an escalator. The men who installed it were totally surprised, but they were all in agreement that Sam Brandeis knew the proper installation procedures at least as well as they did. Sam had them put in extra electric power both upstairs and downstairs so that he and Eva could operate it wherever they were, in the store or in the apartment from whatever room they were in. Sam installed rubber matting on each step so no one would slip while using it. He had to take her up and down on it many times before she felt comfortable enough to use it when he wasn't around.

Sam had an elaborate bell and whistle system put in so that the telephones could be answered wherever anyone who was wanted could speak. He and Eva finally were able to move into the apartment upstairs from the

Manor Bedding Corp. with their son Abraham; a very comfortable arrangement for each of them.

Abe was actually his partner and he had grown into the driving force behind all the manufacturing they did. He made the box springs; he drove each truck the firm owned, one for light deliveries and the one for heavier deliveries. He worked out deals with other manufacturers so that the Manor Bedding Corp. could carry pillows, quilts, mirrors, commodes and small tables.

"We need all this, *Abela*?"

"Why not? Poppa, it is money in the bank. Since when does anyone turn away money, these days?"

"I'm not turning away, *gelt,* my smart son, but I thought we made box springs. We're in the bedding business. You're turning the Manor Bedding Corp. into a grocery store. Soon we'll deliver eggs, bread and butter and milk."

"Not eggs, Poppa, they break. Milk, bread and butter, maybe?"

It was a steady joke between them every time Abe added something new to their merchandise.

Sam was content with his life; his five grandchildren were a badge of success he wore proudly for all to see and would extol each of them to anyone who would listen, friend or stranger, the real and imagined gifts of each.

As the German juggernaut swept through France, Belgium, the Netherlands, Luxembourg, Denmark, Norway and Rumania in 1939 and 1940, Sam Brandeis listened to the news on his radio every night with a terrible lump in his heart. Memories crowded his head. The terrible dread he suffered during his flight from the shtetl returned to upset his sleep many nights. He saw Luca Steiner's body bleeding and lying face down in the water; he heard the screams from the Triangle Fire before he was able to awaken from his nightmare of terror.

He read the Daily Forward, the Jewish newspaper, from cover to cover looking for villages and places and sometimes even names he knew when he crossed half the world to bring Eva and his baby to America. He was particularly interested in Palestine and he read everything he could find in the Forward. Days and nights of the horror of pogroms would awaken him in a cold sweat. Luca Steiner in many forms urged Sam to take his whole family, run and hide, flee or learn to fly.

Sam's uneasiness increased as the German March through Europe couldn't be stopped. When it reached the shores of Dunkirk and the remaining British and French troops had to be evacuated, Sam became convinced that war would reach the shores of the U.S. in short order. Descriptions of the Nazi war machine as being relentless, unstoppable and unbeatable made days and nights far more uncomfortable for those who had risked everything to escape Europe to come to the 'land of the free'. Fearful questions invaded Sam's thoughts and his speech. He verbalized many fears which slowly progressed to become the largest part of his vernacular in both Yiddish and English. The body of Luca Steiner became a frequent visitor to Sam's private thoughts and his uncomfortable dreams.

When Winston Churchill, the Prime Minister of Great Britain, could offer only: "blood, toil, tears and sweat," Sam's hopes for peace sank to its lowest ebb. .

The United States Congress, at the urging of President Roosevelt, passed a budget with millions of dollars geared for defense. When the first peacetime draft began in the United States in October of 1940, Sam fretted about his son *Abela* being drafted into the Army of the United States, marching in foreign countries, looking for an enemy he couldn't see. He imagined rifle shots that reminded him of the one that killed Luca Steiner.

Whenever the Rabbi delivered a speech or a sermon in the synagogue on either a Saturday or a holiday that contained any reference to the war in Europe and its progressive devastation, Sam Brandeis was the first to rise in the defense of his country.

"I didn't bring my wife and tiny baby here, have a family here to grow up to fight and kill and die in

Europe," Sam said. He spoke to many of his customers, his friends in the synagogue and his neighbors. He hated the war with a vehemence that denied the true gentle core of Sam Brandeis.

"In spite of my fears and dislike of guns and wars of any kind for any reason, my family and I will do our part when and if we have to as I'm sure all of you will too. We came here to live in 'the land of the free' and we will do what we have to keep it the 'land of the free'. Our prayers and God will watch over every child and all the others who are called to war."

Part of 1940 and much of 1941became eras of anxiety for most of the American people. Most of them were far from ready for a war. World War I, which was supposed to be 'the war that ended all wars' was constantly brought into conversations. It was offered as proof that "we should mind our own business." Many citizens wondered why Americans should be drawn into another war on another continent without any guarantees that a similar result of World War I would not be the final result again. Pros and cons flew in every conversation. The war in Europe snarled the language with vicious accusations and boiled over into many relationships that ended neighborhood friendships at an alarming rate. Isolationism over committing to a war in Europe seemed to be favored by most of the country's newest citizens.

"The Day of Infamy", December 7, 1941, as articulated by Franklin D. Roosevelt, changed every American life; Sam and his family was no exception.

As the days and nights rolled into months, they were punctuated and highlighted by stories that had war as their main and sometimes only subject. Men in uniform, soldiers and sailors, became a common sight on the streets. Performances of patriotic obligations were indicated by the purchasing of war bonds in support of the efforts to provide our men in service with the best weapons. "Japs" and "Nazis" became the code words for evil. The Italians of Mussolini soon joined them. Heroic feats by any Allied serviceman or woman became headline news for the newspapers and the radio.

Rationing of gas and oil for autos became a prominent part of American lives as they were the most important commodities that were diverted from civilian use to the war effort. Certain foods, such as meat were also rationed as they too were diverted for the use of our troupes. As more and more men were called to the defense of the country, women began to work in factories and industries that were geared toward the war effort.

Gold stars, indicating a death of a son, a brother and sometimes even a father, slowly began to appear in the windows of American homes. Many families were devastated and remained so for years to come.

My friends and I collected silver foil that came from cigarette packages and turned them into an office of the army. We urged our parents to smoke more to further the 'war effort' and even deluded ourselves into believing that we could also help the war effort by becoming a part of the legions of young Americans who started to smoke far too early. We used part of our allowances, if and when they were available to purchase 'war stamps' in school to aid the Allied efforts in Europe.

The grass areas in front of our homes were turned into 'victory gardens', where we planted and grew vegetables that were no longer easily attainable in the neighborhood grocery and fruit stores. We learned to do without many of our favorites as did practically the entire world.

The youngest among us chose up sides and we killed or annihilated every Jap, German and Italian soldier in the world on at least a weekly basis. We fought in the playgrounds, on the streets of the neighborhood, and in and out of our homes when our parents weren't at home. We made up drills so we could march throughout our communities carrying long pieces of lumber that represented our rifles. We built the latest balsa-wood models of the planes our pilots were flying in the air war over European cities. Our marches had more and more significance as gas rationing prevented most families from driving their cars, so that walking to many destinations became more frequent. Our drills prepared us far better than anything our parents did to help them walk any long distances they weren't ready or prepared for.

In school, we lined up for weekly fire drills so that we would be ready for an attack on an American city by any enemy aircraft. We also learned to crawl under our desks when an air raid by the Nazis or the Japs was simulated by the principal of the school that might include bombs to be dropped on our neighborhoods and possibly hit our schools.

In the movies we went to, the American Army, the American Navy and the American Air Force were even more successful at destroying our country's Axis' enemies than we were. In our impressionable young minds, we were able to fight on a dozen fronts at one time and win every battle we engaged in. It never entered our minds that there had to be German, Italian and Japanese young men and women who thought of us at least as the supreme evil in the world as we thought they were and won every war game they invented. During the earliest years of the war, they had much more to be excited about and many more victories to emulate in their imaginations. Of course, we had no idea of how the U.S Press reported our victories or defeats or how the German, Japanese and Italian Press must have reported their progress or defeats.

The athletes we followed on our favorite football and baseball teams were gradually taken into the services and we watched and cheered for their replacements with equal fervor whenever we could get to go to a football game or a baseball game. Dodgers vs. Giants or Yankees vs. any team still drew our boyhood imaginations and loyalties, although not as much as our admiration for our soldiers. War Bond rallies and blood drives were rewarded with tickets to ball games, so we were able to get to go to a ball game every once in a while if we knew a War Bond purchaser or a blood donor.

The 'war effort' became an ominous and constantly thickening cocoon that surrounded our lives. It distilled the ways and meanings of almost every life in America; most certainly every moment that passed during those difficult years was equally affected.

chapter 8

My story

DESPITE THE WAR AND THE painful but necessary sacrifices that it brought to American lives, most people were able to continue on a reasonable path during their daily lives. The gold stars that hung in windows remained a terrible reminder that death had entered a home far too early to be considered reasonable. Parents were putting their children in their final resting places rather than the normal procedure of children putting their parents to rest. Gold stars were becoming more and more commonplace in windows on every block.

Births, graduations, marriages, rites of passage in most religions and normal terminations of life due to either age or serious diseases kept a conventional pace throughout the world that was engaged in a killing war.

My favorite uncle finally lost his exemption as the sole support of his two elderly parents, Sam and Eva, in 1943 and was called to serve his country. Death tolls and seriously wounded American servicemen were rising steadily requiring more men to be called up to serve. There was never any accurate way for us to determine who was actually winning. Stories heard over the radio and read in the newspapers were so slanted that it was impossible for any accurate accounting to be relied upon. The real truth was that the Nazi war machine seemed unstoppable; there were radio announcers and editorial writers who kept that fear like a cancer in the minds of many, many people. There were men and women who expected to find them on our doorsteps at any moment. A combination of enmity and ennui that wrapped many lives was ever present. My friends and I were only interested in enacting and hatching schemes and crazy ideas that would help our country to defeat the 'enemy', whoever that was from any one day to the next.

My parents signed me up to go to Hebrew School in order to study for my Bar Mitzvah. I hated the idea of giving up any afternoons to study for something I didn't want or care about, in another language yet. However, I had no choice nor was there any question that my Bar Mitzvah was a certainty. In our family a ceremonial celebration would occur near or close to a male's thirteenth birthday. It was a necessity that would allow parents, close relatives and some friends to bask in the glow of their son's reaching the birthday in a Jewish boy's life that required special notice be taken. The fact that there was a possibility that if the war lasted long enough, some of my older friends could be called to serve, or even me, was the only unhappy and questionable part of that birthday.

I was the only 'Jewish Kid' in the neighborhood that had to go to school to arrive properly at his thirteenth birthday. I also played the piano, so there was practice every day as well. My father played extraordinarily well and he expected a great deal from me. When I was older, I was sure that his great ability and my limited one was the main factor in my desire to write music rather than play it. My life actually had only small and minor disruptions in it compared to the upheavals and horrors and suffering other families bore in many parts of the world at war.

My grandfather mentioned several times, carefully and deliberately so that I would be sure to hear him, that he expected the *"yeshiva boucher"* ('a student of the Talmudic academy') to observe all the necessities a Jewish boy, who has entered the state of manhood and has been called to the Torah for his Bar Mitzvah would maintain for his lifetime. I knew, and I'm sure Sam Brandeis knew, that the passage of time would erode most promises and many religious practices, from my life. America for many Jewish boys was being folded into more and more American ways which usually left many religious practices by the wayside. It was very difficult for parents who urged English as the spoken tongue of their children and their entry into the mainstream of American life to urge religious observances as well. Sam knew I wasn't going to study to become a Rabbi, so I'm sure we both assumed that with a short period of time, I would shed most of the daily observances but not the practice of the observance of the High Holy Days of Judaism out of respect for my father.

My Bar Mitzvah was celebrated in fine fashion with special gifts from my grandfather, which included a tallis from Israel, an engraved prayer book and a yarmulke that had small studded jewels embossed outlining the six-pointed Jewish Star.

After he allowed me to digest and admire the customary gifts from a doting grandfather to his soon-to-be thirteen year old grandson, he told me he wasn't finished with his presents to me. He had another package in his hand. He handed it to me. It was wrapped in old newspapers tied with the string the Manor Bedding Company used to make box springs.

"Open 'im', *Pitchela Ritchela*. It's for you."

Sam Brandeis had the wonderful twinkle in his eyes together with his suggestive smile indicating that he knew something I didn't know that he could use to tease me with. He handed me a pen knife.

I cut the string from the torn newspapers which

came off with the string. I was holding an oddly shaped box in my hand as the wrappings fell to the floor. I turned the box over and over in my hands. It didn't look like any other shaped box I had ever seen.

One of my fingers found a lever on the top of the box. I pressed it and the top sprang open. On the inside of the top of the box was printed in deep blue capital letters:

PITCHELA -- RITCHELA
GEDAINKIST

Inside the box, on the very bottom were the letters of a man's name and the rank he held in the Kaiser's Private Army. The sides of the box had been sand-papered clean of anything that might have been there before.

I looked at my grandfather; he looked back at me; I had no idea what I was holding. I had never seen a box shaped like this one before.

"This box helped me and your grandmother, Eva, and our two friends Luka Steiner and his wife Rachel escape from our shtetl. We carried it wherever we went and showed it to anyone who asked hostile questions. The name of the man on the bottom of the box was Luca's uncle and a very important man. His name helped us get to a port where we were able to find a boat and a Captain willing to take us to America for a price."

"It is very old, Gram 'pa, and you have saved it a long time. It must be important to you."

"I saved it for the first *'yeshiva boucher'* in the family and that is you. It is yours today. Take good care of it. Never forget you are a Jew."

"What does the other word inside the cover mean?"

"Gedainkist" means 'Remember'."

"I will Gram'pa and I will remember forever. Thank you."

"No other Jewish boy in the world will get such a present because this is the only one of its kind."

"I will keep it and I will remember, Gram'pa, I promise."

One of the benefits that Samuel Brandeis expected from his thirteen-year-old grandson was the recitation of the four questions on the nights of the Seder. I had been reading them in English for five or six years and I knew he was looking forward to my being able to recite them in Hebrew as the youngest male present who had been Bar Mitzvah at the Seder table. He knew that his son Abe had always followed my English recitation in some form of bastardized version of Hebrew without too many questions being raised. The fact that the United States Army was now in charge of his son never left his mind and had made him a sadder man and taken away some of the twinkle in his blue eyes.

On the day of the first Seder, my grandfather

reminded my mother that he expected me to be at his home early enough so that I could join him in the search for anything leavened that he expected to be removed from his home for the entire eight days of Passover. My grandfather and I went through every closet in the house, every bureau drawer and most of the 'nooks and crannies' that might be a secret hiding place for the unwanted leavened food.

"Your Grandmother, Eva, always leaves a few crumbs for me to find, hoping that I will be satisfied with what she has deliberately put in front of my eyes. She hates to give away any food, even to the poor, but she accepts that rather than having anything thrown away, uneaten."

We found crusts of bread as my grandfather said she would have left for him to find. There was also an opened bag of uncooked noodles and some flour that hadn't been used. Sam found some cans underneath clothing in her drawer that were not marked "Kosher for Passover": he greeted each find with a small gasp of triumph. He roared out her name several times letting her know that he had found something she had tried to hide from his eyes.

"Eva, I am saving you from God for not observing the Passover in the way He requires as it is written in the Torah and the Haggadah. You should be happy."

There was more purpose in his search and less fun

than I remembered. My Uncle Abe used to accompany him on these hunts and it was painfully obvious that he knew his son might be in harm's way defending America and not be at home for the hunt and the Seder that night. I was sure I heard him saying Hebrew words quietly as we went through the routine. My mother had warned me that the hunt for good food would be more somber than fun and she was right.

"Whoever throws away good food is crazy," she said as she sent me on my way to Sam's house.

When he was satisfied that he had removed every possible drop of hidden leavened food, he sent me home with a message for my mother that I was to be 'properly dressed' for the Seder. He insisted on a white shirt and a tie under the special tallis he had given me for my thirteenth birthday. I had no problem dressing myself in the exact manner I knew he expected. I rehearsed the 'four questions' a number of times until I felt I would make no mistake at the Seder. I was aware that my Uncle Abe's absence would cause a dampening effect on the whole night and probably would distill most of the humor Sam Brandeis included in the Seders he conducted in his home.

As Sam's children arrived with their husbands and his grandchildren, the weight of the 'missing person' grew heavier with each family arrival. Trying to hold back tears and expressing hopeful wishes was not an easy task for any guest. It was a difficult beginning for all concerned. The empty chair, which my grandfather insisted had to be at the head of the table, was a pointed reminder that we were at war; one of our loved ones was in the United States Army away from our home on this night, the night of the first Seder.

I knew my grandmother's lips were moving in silent prayer as she walked about the kitchen preparing the dinner we would all eat. She chased each of her daughters out of the kitchen, repeatedly reminding them that this was her home and her meal for the Seder.

"Go sit with your husbands and your children and leave my kitchen to me," my Grandmother said. "I can manage this night as well as any night and I can do it better with none of you in my kitchen. Mind your own business and don't eat too many latkes; it's a big dinner for the Seder."

Eva Brandeis made latkes before every Seder; it was a ritual. Each latke weighed a ton before you ate it and two tons as it lay in your stomach. They were very special and defied anyone to eat only one. There were never any 'shortcuts' for Eva Brandeis, on Passover or any other night, no matter what the circumstances.

I watched as Sam inspected the table to make certain everything was exactly as it was called for in the Passover Haggadah he had used for all the years the family was together to celebrate the holiday. Then he called his family to the Seder Table.

He slowly began the proceedings that represented the beginning of the Passover Service. He went through all the rites and ceremonies that were called for to begin the opening of this sacred holiday.

I continued watching him more closely than usual. I was certain that when he rubbed his eyes and complained that the light was too bright causing the tears he was wiping away were tears of worry and longing for his son Abraham.

"We should learn to have our Seders by candlelight, not electric light with large fancy bulbs," I heard him mutter. "When they were in the desert, I don't think God provided the Jews with electricity."

He finally nodded to me that it was time for the four questions. I began to read them in Hebrew for the first time at the Seder. The questions asked why this night was different from all other nights. When I finished, there was almost a trace of a smile on his face that erased the strained look that had begun the night. He grasped my hand under the tallis and said quietly, "Well said, my Grandson, very well said."

His eyes saddened again as he returned to the pages of his Haggadah to begin the answers to the four questions I had asked, which would tell the entire story of Passover as it was told in thousands of Jewish homes throughout the world. There were never any 'short cuts' for Sam Brandeis on Passover, or at any other time he was in conversation with his God, no matter what the additional circumstances.

Sam recited the Passover story as it was printed in his Haggadah, with very few detours or his usual comments on the text. When he reached the recounting of the ten sins God had caused to befall the Egyptians because their Pharaoh had slaughtered Jews and driven those still alive into the desert, he looked up at the ceiling and I heard him say the word "Nazis" quite clearly. He continued his reading and reached the part of the service that called for all those present to eat of the bitter herbs, which were on the plate in the center of the table. He distributed some on pieces of matzah to all those present. We each had a taste of the wine from our glasses lined up on the center of the table.

He gave me an extra portion of horse radish on my piece of matzah, so I too would have tears running down my cheeks. He usually laughed when he looked at my tearful face, but this night he could find no humor in my tears.

"Eva, it is time we washed our hands."

My grandmother brought in a pitcher of water and a basin and all the males present washed their hands as they said a prayer.

"Eva, it is time to eat."

All their daughters rose and went into the kitchen to help serve the Passover meal. Sam sank back on the couch; his body seemed to shrink and disappear, buried in the cushions of the sofa he sat upon. Eating in a reclined position was a symbol of the Jews having no furniture in the desert, forcing them to recline, rather than sit up to eat their evening meal, such as it was.

The women served the meal as their mother handed it to them to be brought to the table.

"Eva, you come too. We will not eat without you. You are in the desert with the rest of us."

Eva came into the dining room and sat on the edge of the couch close to her husband. She tasted each dish and made a comment on each.

"This is better than last year; not bad, but a little salty; something is not right with this; it could be better."

Her daughters assured her that everything was a good as it ever was. Everyone agreed it was delicious. Just as we were all putting the last spoonfuls of food in our mouths, the doorbell downstairs sounded. In a second, there wasn't a sound at the table; no spoons hitting dishes; no knives cutting meat; no movement of moving bodies; only a dreaded silence. Sam looked up and put his arm around his wife. The eerie quiet remained in the dining room; no one stirred. Similar thoughts and dreads went through every mind immediately.

I stood up, opened the door, and took the steps down, two at a time.

I could see a man on the other side of the glass door. He looked like he was dressed in some kind of uniform which I didn't recognize. As I opened the door, he handed me a yellow envelope.

"Telegram for Sam Brandeis. Are you Sam Brandeis?"

"No, sir, I'm his grandson. He's in the middle of the Seder."

"You'll do. You can sign. Just write his name on the line and you sign underneath his name."

He pointed to where I was to sign and handed me the telegram.

I turned the envelope over in my hand. In the dim light, I was sure I could see that the telegram was from the United States War Department.

"Just a moment, please sir."

He nodded and I started back up the stairs, gripping the envelope in my hand.

"I need a quarter, quick," I said. I went back down without giving the telegram to anyone. I knew it had to be opened and read but I was terrified of its contents.

I gave the messenger the quarter.

"Best of luck," he said and disappeared into the black night. I closed the door and turned to run back up the stairs. My mother was standing at the top of the stairs.

I gave her the telegram. She opened it; I envisioned a gold star hanging in the window of The Manor Bedding Corp.

She cried out a desperate "No," and threw the telegram on the table. "Abie, Abie, no, no, not my brother."

I picked up the paper and read aloud from it. It said, "We regret to inform you that your Son, Abraham Brandeis, has been slightly wounded in the service of his country."

There was no more information other than those words. There was a promise of further communication when it became available.

Eva screamed heart-rending words I had never heard before in Yiddish. She collapsed in a heap on the couch. Her daughters picked her up and took her into the bedroom. She remained inconsolable. The men didn't know how to react. They stared at Sam and each went to him to try to assure him that his son would be okay. Screams continued to come from the darkened bedroom. No one in the dining room could be quite sure who they came from. Every once in a while one of the daughters came out of the bedroom to clear the table of what was left of the Passover dinner.

The men walked into the living room, equally stunned. They did not know what they were supposed to do or what the correct behavior called for. They talked quietly and inevitably re-told stories of other families they knew who had received telegrams from the War Department with far greater tragic events in their contents.

I sat at the table with my grandfather, uncertain of any words that I should say to ease the pain of the telegram. It was a dreadfully helpless feeling.

He picked up the telegram and stared at the words on the paper. He looked at me through eyes that were not his eyes.

"This is how they tell you something like this? On this night when we ask God, "How different is this night from all other nights?"

I had never seen him look like he did at that moment. There was a terrible hurt in his eyes that was indescribable.

"Gram'pa, it says 'slightly wounded'. It cannot be too serious. Abie is okay, gram'pa, he's okay. 'Slightly wounded.' it says. He's okay, gram'pa. I know it."

I read the telegram to him again.

"He's alive, gram'pa. Remember *'Dayenu'!* (It is enough.)" I had spoken the Hebrew word that we had used in the prayer when describing the ten plagues God had wrought on the Egyptians.

"DAYENU! Is it really enough? We can only hope and pray it is enough and that it is true, that telegram.

Who knows? It is nice that the American Government found the time to tell us that."

Sam fell back among the cushions on the couch after pushing away the meal he would no longer finish.

"My poor son Abie is living in the desert with his own plagues. God, you will watch."

The last few words sounded like a command to me.

A sound came from deep within him as the terrible truth of the Government's telegram registered in its full force. It hit him hard directly in the gut. Sounds of despair continued coming from the bedroom where all the women of the family were still trying to calm their mother and themselves from the abyss the telegram had brought with it.

Sam suddenly sat up. He reached behind one of the pillows and brought out the matzah he had placed there at the beginning of the Seder Service.

"My grandson, we will finish the Seder Service together, you and me. God must not think we have abandoned Him because we might think he has abandoned us."

There were never any short cuts for Sam Brandeis, no matter what the circumstances.

He handed me a piece of that matzah and took one for himself. It was dry and hard to swallow. He looked at me and I stared at him.

"You can drink some wine from your glass with this matzah."

We both took our cups from the center platter where they stood for the Seder and sipped enough to wash down the piece of matzah.

He pointed to the rest of the glasses that had remained on the tray at the center of the table. Some were emptied and some were half-filled. The tallest glass was completely filled as it had been for the entire service.

"We will stand; then you will go and open the door. After that, you will come back to the table. The Prophet Elijah will enter through the door you have opened. He will drink from only one cup, his cup, the tallest one still full in the center of the tray."

I went to the door and opened it as he had instructed. I returned to the table and stood beside him. I didn't have anything that was akin to his faith, but this was not the time to engage in any discussion about what Sam Brandeis believed or my thoughts about opening the door. Sam picked up his Haggadah and began a prayer slowly and almost impossible for me to hear even though I was standing next to him. Quite suddenly, the wine in the tallest glass moved. It seemed that someone or something had taken a sip from it. I did not believe what I saw, but I have lived the rest of my life knowing with an absolute certainty that the tallest cup in the center of the table had moved at that moment as if someone had taken a sip from it.

I looked at my grandfather. The muscles in his face relaxed; there was a trace of satisfaction on his face for the first time since the dreaded telegram had arrived.

"You can close the door now, *Pitchela Ritchela*. Elijah has been here. The empty chair will soon be filled; it will not be empty forever. God is watching over Abie: all is well."

He closed his Haggadah and slowly removed his tallis.

chapter 9

Segue

Before the second night of Passover and the second Seder, Sam told me he wanted to learn how to write in English so he could communicate with his son. He told me that he expected me to do that for him as quickly as was humanly possible. It was not a great effort for me as I was at the Manor Bedding Corp. several times a week anyway. My father had set up a simplified bookkeeping system as soon as my Uncle Abe went into the service so that the business would have records that would allow it to file whatever tax returns were required for the running of its business.

It was not a hardship for me to show up as often as I did. We lived close enough so it was a short walk between our homes. I also considered it part of my contribution to the war effort as I was performing a dual function for my grandfather, my uncle and the Manor

Bedding Corp. Therefore, the war effort of the United States was being served as well.

Sam learned to write capital letters in English very quickly. His printing was large but he didn't care. As long as he was able to 'write to my Abie', his purpose was completely served. As it said in the Passover service: *"DAYENU"*; it was most certainly enough.

There is no way there was any form or combination of letters that I knew to use to describe his joy when he received an answer from his son to the first letter he had mailed himself. Abraham Brandeis had been 'slightly wounded' in "The Battle of the Bulge", which his letter to his father partially explained. A short hospital stay was all that was required. It became almost a turning point of the war as the Nazi war machine began to deteriorate appreciably following that battle.

Thus began a correspondence between two unlikely family members that resulted in a highly rare and lovely exchange that lasted until Private Abraham Brandeis was mustered out of the United States Army.

Sam made certain rules I had to follow:

1. I had to inspect his writing of the alphabet every time we sat down to learn. (He wrote every letter of the entire alphabet in caps, forcing himself to learn the correct order of all the letters).
2. He had to go through the Jewish paper he read (the Daily Forward) and from it he would

generate the questions he wanted to ask his son that did not relate to his health.

3. He was also a fervent follower of one of the newscasters on the radio – Gabriel Heater – who would open each program every night with the words: 'there's good news tonight" or "there's bad news tonight." From those words Sam would formulate the body of his letter to his son. (I think more than half of America followed those words and the tenor of Americans' conversation would reflect them the very next day – sadness or elation).

(It was during our going over Mr. Heater's words and Sam's perusal of "The Daily Forward" that I learned of his deep devotion to Palestine and the Jews. He would pause whenever there was a column or a reference to a Jewish homeland or the killing of Jews anywhere in the world. He would stop and speak out against the violence and the need for all Jews to have 'a place to rest their bones without worrying about their family's lives or their own.' Sam never expressed a desire to go to or live in Palestine. He just wanted all Jews to have a choice of a place of their own so they could no longer be driven from where they were to 'God knows where'. He spoke against the Nazis with a bitterness I didn't know he possessed.)

"My friend Luca Steiner and thousands of other Jews

who fled from the pogroms might still be alive today if they had a place like Palestine to go to, instead of having to cross thousands of miles populated by people who hated them to get to a boat that went to America."

To celebrate his son's return to the United States, Sam built a huge sign on a framed plywood board. My family's brick one-family home was the only one where he could hang and electrify the sign properly. He painted it red, white and blue, bought red, white and blue bulbs and wired it so that they blinked on and off when a button was pressed. He printed his son's name himself and painted each letter red, white or blue but his whole name stayed lit from the day Sam finished the sign until he embraced his son on his return to US soil.

No doubt, the sign created some unrest among families in our neighborhood that had lost a loved one in the war, but somehow, if it was spoken about, our family never heard it.

After the second war, 'to end all wars' formally ended on the European Continent, two atomic blasts on Japanese soil brought them to a full surrender.

Life for my family slowly started to return to some form of the normalcy it had engaged in before the war began. We were not unique; the rest of the country and the world that had been killing each other for so long, gradually resumed living in a restive peace, re-dedicating itself to rebuilding and moving forward and out of the hysterical abyss the war created.

My Uncle Abe returned fully recovered from his wound. He went out with several women and finally met a woman he cared for. They married (I was best man) and gradually set up housekeeping in their own apartment, leaving the entire apartment over the Manor Bedding Company to my grandparents. They had two new arrivals in a short space of time, both girls who happily added to the size of the Brandeis clan.

As one branch of the family increased, two other families moved out of New York State. Mildred's family moved to Providence Rhode Island as the demands of employment of the head of their household was governed by a shift in his employer's headquarters to that city. They eventually moved again, this time to Philadelphia as the firm her husband worked for made him a manager in their newest store there. Celia's family moved much further; Los Angeles California was their destination in search of more and better opportunities as new industries opened in California. The move to California eventually lead to another move, this one to Hawaii, just before it became the forty-ninth state of the Union.

Sam and Eva Brandeis could now proudly count seven grandchildren among their family spread across the country.

chapter 10

My Story

B Y MY TWENTIETH BIRTHDAY AN unusual discontent seem to come over me. I had been studying to become an accountant and I hated it. I decided to quit going to college. I sincerely wanted to compose music. I had written the music for two shows in college and I decided that I was going to compose for the rest of my life. My parents were beside themselves with my decision. Argument followed argument; it was like a cancer feeding upon itself and becoming uglier and uglier. I decided I would check into aiding in the fight for a Jewish homeland in Palestine.

I had to give a few piano lessons to generate some income for myself. It wasn't easy. A few well designed circulars under every door in the neighborhood and I was able to contact a few students. I made enough money to pay for some enjoyments to ease the pain of the existence I had chosen. Starving composers were far more glamorous to me than well-to-do accountants. My parents refused to support any of my activities.

"Back to college, study accounting, pass the C.P.A. exam or no money," became the mantra by which they lived.

I was at the Manor Bedding Corp. visiting with my grandfather, when the realization that Sam was growing older almost as fast as my parents and I were growing apart, dictated to me that I spend more time with him. His main topics of conversation beside the pleasantries we exchanged were the holocaust, the tremendous difficulties in Palestine and the ongoing discussions in the United Nations about statehood for a Jewish nation in Palestine.

I had no difficulty remembering that when he was learning to write English words to his son, much of his reading matter, besides being about the war in Europe, was usually related to Jews being slaughtered or threatened with annihilation by the various countries they happened to be living in at any given time. When the holocaust numbers were able to be sustained, proven and published after the Allies overran the German war machine in Europe, he became more involved with organizations in the United States that were sworn to help the Jews. He provoked his friends into giving money; he stood tall in his synagogue and spoke about the need for donating for Palestine as well as donating to keep the synagogue going. The Manor Bedding Corp.'s best customers were harangued to the point of Abe asking him to tone it down to preserve their customer list.

"Easy poppa or we will be selling milk and eggs and bread and butter."

"One day, we will sell them to Jews in Palestine, my son. Not to worry."

Sam Brandeis knew or was aware of nearly every organization, association, brotherhood or group, Jewish or otherwise that was in any way connected to the case of a homeland in Palestine for the Jewish people. I knew that I could go to him for information I wanted relating to finding an active organization that would be able to put me in direct touch with anyone that might be able to send me to Palestine to be of some aid in the Jews' drive for their own land. I had no way of knowing what his response might be to such a request. I had no one else to turn to unless I launched an extensive search that might take weeks or longer assuming that it was successful.

He spoke to me at length after he listened carefully to everything I had to say, including my request. I could see in his eyes that he was pleased but the look on his face was quite the contrary. There was doubt written across it about his willingness to become a part of the plan I had outlined to him.

"*Ritchela*, this is an admirable idea but along with its

commendable thought, you are putting a great burden on my shoulders. You must know and understand that I have no desire to send my grandson into a situation that might cause him great harm, or, perhaps, even worse. Let us imagine for a moment that your parents have a similar desire as yours for a place in this world that every Jew can call "home." God forbid I go along with your request and the result is not as you foresee it. Where would I go in my own broken heart for forgiveness and then face your parents and have to deal with the result that you came to a bad ending and I helped you get there?"

Of course I was more than ready for his thinking about a tragic outcome that can be traced to his decision to grant my request.

"Sometimes in life, Gram'pa, as you have said to me many times, a situation arrives that requires only one answer: 'put up or shut up'. That situation and that time is right now for me."

"I can see your point but, "putting up or shutting up" with your own life is not the same as offering another life that is not your own to "put up or shut up". There can be no doubt that a wonderful idea can come to a bad ending, especially in a case that concerns differences of opinions that are being settled by guns. I have to consider that a possibility if I grant you your request."

"Gram'pa, you are only giving me a chance to

get where I want to go with a minimum of checking and calling and calling some more. You will only be reducing my search time. This is where I am in my life. I have given this a great deal of thought and I really want to participate in the struggle for a Jewish homeland. I only want to use the connections I know you have to save myself all that effort. Gram'pa, it is my decision; I'm going to get to Palestine one way or the other. That is not a threat; it is a reality for me."

"Have you mentioned this idea to either of your parents?"

"No, I have not. I intend to talk to them when I know that I am capable of doing what I want to do. That means when the "red tape" is no longer a part of my decision. I am twenty years old and my life decisions are actually mine to make. There can be no blame attached to that, only mine. Gram'pa, to be honest, I'm going to do this with or without your help. My mind is made up."

"That kind of talking tells me you are not nearly as grown up as you think you are. You have ignored that sometimes your decisions can cause great pain to others. Most ideas have consequences, sometimes even unintended consequences that might affect lives that have not had any part of the consummation of that idea. Recognizing and dealing with those consequences is an important part of the maturation process in young adults."

It was suddenly quiet, very quiet. There was no more talking as we each framed another response in defense of our thoughts. We obviously wanted our next words to be the final words in this conversation.

My Grandfather broke the uneasy silence.

"I would like a little more time to collect all my thoughts," he said quietly. He talked to me and squeezed my hand, as he had the night of the Seder.

"I will not take long, I promise."

"Thank you. I know there are many, many people and organizations whose sympathies lie with the founding of a Jewish State. I will find them. Without any disrespect to you, Gram'pa, I will find them and use them to fulfill my mission."`

"You just have to promise me that you will discuss this with your parents."

"You have my solemn promise I will do that before I make any final arrangements concerning Israel."

"Good. *Dayenu, Pitchela Ritchela.*"

A few days later my grandfather gave me a lined piece of paper, obviously left over from his days as a correspondent. I looked at the three telephone numbers he had written. There were no names of people or organizations, just the numbers.

"Use the numbers; one of them will have the answers you are searching for. Please tell whoever answers your call exactly what you want. The first number is probably the best. You may use my name on each call. Throw away what you don't use.

I knew he wouldn't have given me the numbers if he didn't agree with my proposal or at least want me to follow it to some conclusion. He must have decided I would start looking on my own and he wanted me to be connected to the best. I did not see his confirmation of my desires in his supplying the list to me.

When I contacted the first number on the list, the voice at the other end asked me who I was and how I got the telephone number. When I mentioned Sam Brandeis, the voice told me to hang up and call back the very next day as soon as I opened my eyes whatever the hour. The entire conversation took less than a minute; the voice at the other end had somehow made me feel that I was in the right place. I put off calling the other numbers. I believed I had found exactly what I was looking for.

I called the same number the next day at 6:10 AM. A different voice answered.

"Who are you?"

I gave the voice my name.

"Where or who did you come from?"

I gave the voice my Grandfather's name.

"One moment please."

There was a prolonged silence with absolutely no

sound from the other end of the telephone. The same voice from my first phone call came into my ear.

"Do you have a paper and pencil handy?"

"Yes I do."

"Copy what I say."

I heard a distinctly Hebrew name; the voice gave me the correct spelling of the name.

"Please say the name."

I did the best I could.

"That's close enough. Tomorrow you will report here at 7AM sharp," the voice said. "Repeat the name."

I did.

I was about to ask "where" when the voice came back into my ear and said, "What you and I and Sam Brandeis have spoken about must remain between the three of us. Be very sure."

"Yes sir."

"Good. When you arrive, ask for the name you repeated."

"I will."

"Tomorrow at 7AM sharp you will come alone. After you have asked for the name I gave you, someone will lead to the room *chai*. *Chai* is LIFE in Hebrew. The mystic numeric number that has been assigned to chai is 18. Room 18 is where you will go. If you are truly authentic, Sam Brandeis will call you at home and give you the address of where you are to go tomorrow, where room *chai* is located. Do you have any questions?"

I thought for a moment. I was confused, but I had no questions, especially if my grandfather was going to call me.

"No questions."

I heard the click in my ear as the telephone at the other end was returned to its cradle.

The entire telephone call remained a mystery to me until long after I met with the people who I had been searching for. I assumed that whoever they were had to be sure I was really related to Sam Brandeis; that had to be the reason for getting the correct address directly from him. I believed everything else in the conversation had been used to cover whatever they thought had to be covered for their security. Obviously they wanted their actions to be as private and secret from prying eyes, sharp ears and unfriendly voices. I thought that everything would be made clear to me once I was accepted into their group. The underlying acceptance of whatever they wanted or did was, of course, my firm belief in Sam Brandeis.

The address he gave me was a small hotel on the West Side of Manhattan. The sun had not yet risen and in the cavern of buildings I was in, I was sure I wouldn't be able to see any more clearly for another hour; it was only ten minutes to seven. I had never realized there was a hotel this far West on any street in Manhattan. I double checked the address Sam had given me on a lined piece of paper left over from his correspondence with his son. The handwriting was unmistakably his; so was the lined paper. I found the name of the hotel emblazoned on one of the door panels almost hidden from view. Another precaution?

I opened the door to the lobby. I entered a large, spare and worn-looking room. I walked to what I took for granted served as a reception area.

A small, wizened woman with her graying hair tied in a messy bun behind her neck sat behind a long table set up on two horses that served as a desk. She looked up at me. Her eyes narrowed as she adjusted thin wire-framed glasses on the end of her pointed nose. She returned to reading the newspaper that was spread out on the table she was sitting behind. I stood quietly waiting for her to speak to me.

"Damned British bastards," I heard her mutter.

The curse was clearly hissed with venom and laced with hatred. I was sure I was in the right place.

She looked up at me again and folded the newspaper and put it to one side of the table which was piled high with papers.

"You looking for someone in particular?"

"Yes, I am."

I repeated the name the person I originally spoke to

gave me. The woman repeated the name loudly, with a decided accent on the last syllable.

"That's the way he pronounces it."

"Thank you. I will remember the proper pronunciation."

I showed her the paper I had written the name on.

"You got the spelling right. What's your name?"

"Richard."

I was about to say my surname, but she held up a boney hand.

"No last names yet, Richard. Sit on that red chair over there. I'll see if he's in yet and expecting you."

I walked to the red chair and sat down. The woman was speaking on the telephone. I looked around the dingy, poorly lit room. The walls and the ceiling were decidedly in need of a scraping and several coats of paint. One rug barely covered half the floor of the room; it was frayed at the edges and threads lay on the floor where they were hanging from the sides of the rug. The two windows in the room were caked with dirt and effectively hid prying eyes from the alley that ran along one of the outside walls of the hotel. One could not see out from the inside either. There was a permeating, stale odor of the constant traffic that the room was a party to. The red chair I was seated in also had an odor coming from it. I moved closer to the edge and waited.

The woman hung up the phone and looked at me.

"Sit back and make yourself comfortable," she said in a voice that was modulated perfectly to be heard exactly where I was seated.

"It'll be about five minutes."

I had no intention of moving any deeper on the cushion of the chair; I waited.

A tall man, wearing a yarmulke appeared at one end of the table. He spoke to the woman, turned in my direction as she pointed me out to him and started to walk towards me. I stood up and stared at him.

His face was pale, almost bereft of color. His eyes, however, were a striking black, even made blacker by the whiteness of the sclera. The combination of his eyes and pale face gave him the appearance of a Halloween costumed face. He extended a hand with long boney fingers which led me to think they would serve any musician well. I took his hand in mine; it was icy cold.

"Shalom, Richard. I am Chaim. Please follow me."

His introduction, without a last name evidently was in keeping with the code of the organization.

He dropped my hand and turned back to the long table. He said a few words to the woman which I could not hear clearly. It didn't matter because they were all in Hebrew. Then he turned and motioned to me to follow him. He led the way down a long, dark corridor to a door marked "elvator". Someone must have needed the other "e" because one was missing from the word elevator.

The elevator was as unkempt as the parts of the building I had already seen. As it started to rise, it sounded as if the machinery that made it work was dying a horrible death. It stopped on the tenth floor; the door creaked open slowly. Chaim exited first and turned to make sure I was following him. He stopped in front of a door marked *"CHAI"*.

Chaim knocked, waited to be invited in and opened the door to a well-lit room. The sun streamed in from the spotless windows which had no curtains on them. There were stacks of books and papers almost from floor to ceiling everywhere. An old metal desk stood in one corner of the room, behind which were seated an elderly woman and a man with a thick black beard that covered most of his face and flowed down far enough on his chest to cover the knot of his tie. He had on a black fedora barely perched on the back of his head. His face was one of those that looked like a constant smile was painted on it. I thought it was a great pleasure and in contrast to everyone else I had seen that early in the morning. He rose from behind the desk.

"Shalom."

I believed it was time that I should get used to that greeting.

"Shalom."

He shook my hand.

"We will not use proper names until we are all certain that we are in agreement with the tasks ahead."

"I figured that out, sir."

He was a little shorter than I was but he must have weighed at least fifty pounds more than I did. He was dressed in a creased black suit that was not pressed and as black as his beard and Chaim's eyes. The fedora on top of his head was also black and pushed back as far as it would go without falling backward off his head. I had expected him to be wearing a tallis, but I was disappointed. It made me even more aware that I was now in a separate and strange world. My feelings as to where I was, who I might meet there or what I might find there, didn't matter. I expected to be ready for as many surprises as might come.

He pointed to the woman still seated behind the desk.

"This woman is my compatriot. You will get to know each of us with names and other facts when we have completed outlining our arrangements and you have agreed to abide by them. Please have a seat."

The woman nodded to me and went back to whatever she had been doing when I came into the room. I sat down on a hard, unpadded metal chair. The man pulled up a similar chair and sat facing me.

SURPRISE #1

"How is Brandeis?"

"He's well, thank you."

SURPRISE #2

"I have known Sam for a great many years."

"Really?"

"That's true. I would guess that it was pretty soon after he moved with Eva and their baby from the East Side of Manhattan to Brooklyn," he continued. "I recall him practicing at making box springs.

"I am a graduate Rabbi, complete with all the trappings that go with it. Even today, it is a very, very difficult way to make a decent living. I bought into a furniture store on Utica Avenue, in Brooklyn."

"I know where that is."

"Sam learned more and more about making box springs. He worked for a bedding firm for a little while and then, I heard he went out for himself. During the war, Sam continued to supply me with the only steel box springs in the all of Brooklyn. I don't know how or where he got them from. I never asked him; it was none of my business. He kept me supplied during the war and, as a matter of fact, I think I was the only entrepreneur in Brooklyn that was able to sell a box spring made with real steel springs. Sam drove his finished springs right to my store, insisted on unloading them all and carrying them into the store himself.

'It's part of the service', he said whenever someone tried to help him."

"I can tell you sir, that his son, my Uncle Abe, made every single one of those box springs while he still had an exemption from the United States Army. I never asked, either, where or how he got the steel springs."

The man seemed satisfied that I had corroborated his part of the Sam Brandeis story.

"I understood his son was wounded during the fighting in Europe."

"My Uncle Abe returned from the war in one piece. He came home safely, got married and is raising a family of his own. He still works and he's Sam's partner in the Manor Bedding Co. on Coney Island Avenue in Brooklyn."

"That's good, very good. It's a pleasure to hear a story about the recent war that has a happy ending to it. It seems very difficult to come upon now-a-days."

I nodded and waited for him to start on whatever was expected of me.

"I'll make this as short as possible. There is a certain protocol that must be followed. I'm pretty sure that a war is on the near horizon for the Jews, no matter how the vote in the UN Assembly goes."

"I'm really sorry to hear that, but unfortunately I agree with you."

"There is an application of sorts you must fill out,

as if you were actually applying for a job in New York. It indicates the usual; name, age (ultra important if you need parental approval)."

"I just celebrated my twentieth birthday."

"Good, very good. We don't need parental approval then, a step that blocks many of our recruiting efforts. Jewish Parents, no matter how strong their feelings may be for Palestine seem to be, shall I say 'sticky' about their children going there during these difficult times; damn the British. There are other little details that are necessary: do you have a valid American passport; can you be away from the USA for any length of time without your parents calling the FBI; estimate the dates you may be available; do you speak and/or write and understand Hebrew; will a boat trip make you sea-sick (etc.etc.etc.) There are other minor details. However, I find it is far easier if you come across anything troubling to you or that you cannot answer, just ask. By the way, it is still "Palestine" to me.

The woman behind the desk handed him several sheets of paper, which he rifled through briefly and then handed to me. He gave me a pen.

"Before you start, it is ultra important that you know that there is about a week of training, if your application is accepted. Nothing strenuous, mostly minor stuff, the most important of which is learning to use a rifle; how to aim it, shoot it and becoming familiar enough with it to take it apart and put it back together in absolute blackness. You will also be taught about Palestine, its terrain and geography. I'm sure a few important words in Hebrew might be thrown in, in case of an emergency and you are all alone somewhere."

"I understand."

"I'll go into greater detail when you have finished the application and answered any questions you might ask. The training is not conducted in New York City."

"No objections, so far."

"Complete as much as you can and give it to my compatriot behind the desk. If you have any questions, you may ask her. If everything is okay, we'll go on in greater detail, as I said, and all questions will be answered to each of our total satisfaction."

He stood up, straightened the hat on the top of his head, shook hands with me, nodded to the woman behind the desk and left the room.

I left the city, five hectic days later for a place indicated to me only as 'upstate'. I had no problem with that; I was glad to finally get started on my journey. The man I met the first day, Chaim, picked me up in his truck, stopped for two other young people and drove upstate.

I sat next to him in the cab; the others were sprawled out on the mattresses in the back. After several hours of slow, very careful driving, Chaim pulled up in front of a building which was perched on the top of a small rise. It was a dormitory and probably was where we would live during our training. When I got out, I was able to see fallow land going all the way to the horizon in every direction.

We joined about ten other young men and women who, I assumed, were quartered in the same building. I was very happy they led us to what served as a cooking and eating room. I was famished; the only stops along our route were bathrooms.

Males were separated from females by another large room which was known as the 'learning' room.

The only restrictions that were placed on us were that we had to be wherever we were instructed to be at the exact time we were told to be there. It took several days, but we were all living together easily and, I might say, happily.

Our rifle instructor was a tall, limber, muscular woman who fairly obviously wore no underclothes beneath her blouse. She was the talk of most of the young males in the group and projected an immense amount of wonder and conjecture. Her red hair was tied in a pony tail and it seemed to fly apart from the rest of her body when she walked. She rarely smiled, seemed all business-like. She smoked cigarettes continuously, sometimes even lighting one from the stub of her last cigarette. The only human contact I had with her was when she demonstrated the "prone position" and I didn't get truly prone. She walked to where I was lying, jumped on my posterior with both feet and then slapped me on the head.

"Down is down," she said, "learn it or your head will be blasted off your shoulders. I don't particularly care about your head; it's whoever is next to you who will be left unprotected if your ass is in pieces the sky."

When I told her I couldn't close my left eye so as to aim correctly in the prone position, she ordered a patch for that eye. When she adjusted it around my head and on my left eye, she pulled it and let go of it so that it snapped into place on my face. I felt the sting.

"I want to see that patch in place whenever you have a rifle in your hand."

She began calling me "Moishe" when I did anything wrong and "Dayan" when I did anything she approved of. Each name stuck with me during the entire time I was involved with the group, both here and later on foreign soil.

In the "learning room" we had almost all male instructors except when we had to practice taking our rifles apart and putting them back together in the dark. It was the same tall, limber woman, who was just as provocative in the "learning room" as she was out on the rifle range. Surprisingly to me, she never called me "Moishe", but only "Dayan" in the darkened room. I began to feel a special familiarity and bond growing between us. The rest of the instructors were men who showed us the geography and the terrain of Israel. We became familiar with the names of the "kibbutzim" that had been in what was then Palestine for many years. We learned several important words and names in Hebrew, should we get into a situation where they might be helpful and useful. When the classes were over those of us who had driver's licenses and were not familiar with 'shift cars' were given an opportunity to practice on them and learn how to drive them smoothly.

Toward the evening of every day, just before a supper meal was served, each one of us had a private conference with a different instructor from one of the leadership positions. I had no way of knowing, but it seemed we were each being assessed to determine how we could be best used and where and what that might be in the service of Palestine.

During our last experience with our rifles in the blackness of the learning room, our red-headed instructress stopped at my side, leaned over me, put a piece of paper in the pocket of my shirt and walked away without saying a word.

I nearly exploded with excitement until I was able to get to the privacy of my dorm room to read what was on the paper she slipped into my pocket. It was an invitation to join her outside on the North side of the building one hour after the lights had been turned out for the night. It took me but a few moments to find one of my cohorts who knew north from south and east from west, all the while wondering "why me?".

When I closed the door to the dorm behind me, I could see the glow of her cigarette in the inky, black night. I walked quickly to her side. She dropped the cigarette, crushed it beneath her heel and pushed me firmly against the side of the building. Her lips pressed against mine and some of the residue of the cigarette entered my mouth along with her tongue. I couldn't breathe.

Her hand slipped down the front of my pants and found my erection. I felt my knees grow weak from her touch.

"Come with me, quickly."

Without releasing me, she led me to a spot behind a small grove of trees. It was dark but I could make out the shape of her body. There was a blanket on the ground. She let go of me, took off her blouse and skirt and stood naked in the night except for her shoes. I felt my heart pound as I stared at what I had been imagining since I saw her the first day on the rifle range. I stopped wondering "why me".

Her breasts were truly beautiful; I had never seen anything like them in my young life. Her body was like not the bodies I had ogled in the darkness of my bedroom in the nude magazines I had hidden at the bottom of a dresser drawer. Every curve was sensual and the composite picture emanated a sexual power I had never felt, seen or experienced before. I reached out to touch her but she caught my hand in mid-air.

"Not yet, Dayan. Take your clothes off first. You must learn to act like a gentleman. There is time," she commanded.

She curled her body on the blanket and watched me as I took my clothes off. She turned on her back when I was naked and stretched her arms out to me. She pulled me down onto the blanket, gripped my penis again and guided it to her vagina.

"OK, my young warrior, now show me you have finally learned the correct prone position and how to use it."

When I was inside her, she locked her legs tightly around my back halting any movement I was trying desperately to make. She held me for what seemed an eternity and then relaxed her legs. I exploded inside her far too quickly.

"Don't worry or be ashamed. I can make your body do what I want it to do. Next time and the next time and the next time, it will be much slower and much more enjoyable for both of us."

She took turns lighting a cigarette and making love to me. The flame of her cigarette lighter illuminated her body and I drank it in until each cigarette was lit. One act followed immediately after the other. I don't know how long we were together on the blanket. She had an iron control over my body; she took it places it had never been before. Wonder of wonders, I was never exhausted enough so that I could not respond almost immediately to her driving, unquenchable desire.

"Dayan, I have liked everything about you since day one, especially the way you handled the eye patch. I believe that you are the oldest in years, but also the oldest in the way I have perceived you think and act. I have to deal with too many youngsters who I believe are not really ready for any type of the missions required by this organization. In these hellish times there is no room for trial and error, or too many questions. I hope I have spoiled you for every woman that comes after me and there will be many, many."

I wasn't quite sure exactly what she meant until many years later.

At the first sliver of light in the sky she sprang up from the blanket.

"When you return from your adventure, Dayan, whatever it may be please don't come back here to look for me. I will not be here, in any case. I would rather keep you as my delicious, very private memory. Goodbye and good luck."

She dressed, rolled up the blanket, lit a cigarette,

smiled at me and was gone. I cannot enumerate the number of times I saw her nakedness in my mind. She had left a picture in my head that seemed to diminish the nakedness and the sexual drive of all the other women in my less than adult life.

On what was supposed to be the last day 'upstate', I was called into a conference by the same man I had met at the hotel in New York City.

SURPRISE #3

"Well, *Pitchela Ritchela*, what do you think of all this. Oh, by the way, regards from Sam Brandeis."

"Thank you, sir."

He extended his hand and accepted mine warmly between his two hands. His use of my grandfathers' special name for me I hope meant some sort of approval for what I was embarking on from Sam or he would not have shared that name with anyone.

"You have done well and we have picked out a most important project for you to execute. By the way, my name is Jacob Ben-Menachem. Sam already shared your special name with me. I hope you don't mind."

"If he told it to you, either he was very sure of you or he finally reached a spark of approval for what I am doing."

"A little bit of each, I'm sure."

chapter 11

Sam's Story

WHEN HE FINALLY GAVE A special telephone number to his grandson, Sam recognized the slow return of a familiar knot in his stomach. He could not help recalling the days and nights of distress he experienced when his son, Abe, was called to the service of his country. The agony of "not knowing" gradually returned and his days were filled with a gnawing feeling of uncertainty.

His friend Jacob Ben-Menachem told him that communication with his grandson was impossible. His destination or his whereabouts would not be disclosed to anyone and the nature of what he was involved in was a deeply held secret. There were to be absolutely no exceptions.

"Sam, please believe me, I am not sure of anything concerning your grandson either," Jacob said when Sam called him to find out if there was anything new.

"You must remember that I am only a small cog in a wheel with many spokes. I am more involved with recruiting and teaching than I am with plans, strategy or locations. Everyone has his or her forte and we respect each other and the pledge we made to not speak about our roles or the organization to anyone."

Sam had no choice but to accept all the conditions Jacob Ben-Menachem had advised him would be necessary for him to disclose to Sam the information he asked about to provide to his grandson. Sam consoled himself with the knowledge that Richard could have called any well-known organization similar to the B'nai Brith or many others and they would have put him in touch with the help he wanted and needed to send him on his way to completing his venture.

"I am saving him valuable time that I am sure will be well spent," was his mantra when his apprehensions seemed to overwhelm him.

Sam knew, unfortunately, that there was a day looming in the very near future when he would receive a phone call from his daughter '*Channa*', Richard's mother. He had no way of knowing what might have been said between parents and child because his grandson refused to discuss it with him.

"There was a great deal of tension between them and me at the time, Gram'pa. They wanted me to go back to school. I said I wouldn't and then I told them I would be going on a trip to Israel and there was no talking about it. It was my decision and that was that. I refused to talk about it anymore."

Sam felt he would be held responsible for any decisions his grandson might arrive at that remotely touched upon anything Jewish. Sam's interest in Palestine as a homeland for Jews had been a vocal part of his life since his flight with Eva to America, the death of Luca Steiner and the appalling actions of the rest of the world allowing the Nazi Holocaust to occur. He appreciated the fact that no amount of rehearsing platitudes would save him from her anger and allow him to give her an answer that would satisfy both her and Richard's father. The only antidote he knew of was a safe and early return by their son and he had as much control over that as Jacob Ben-Menachem had indicated he had: absolutely none.

Sam resumed his habit of reading the Jewish Daily Forward. He searched its pages for news of Palestine, Israel, the UN, the Arab League and anything else that might allow him to get closer to where his grandson might be and what he might be involved in. There was no Gabriel Heater on the radio who could advise him: "There's good news tonight" or "There's bad news tonight".

He made many phone calls to people he knew who were heavily invested and sympathetic to the Jewish struggle, but he was only able to hear rumors at the other end; rumors that had as much truth in them as the Yiddish saying: *az di bobe volt gehat beytsim volt zi geven mayn zeyde* (If my grandmother had testicles, she would be my grandfather). He smiled every time he thought of the saying. He had used it himself many, many times in conversations with customers who suggested he lower his prices so as to make a better bargain for themselves on a product from the Manor Bedding Company they wanted to buy.

Two days later, Richard's parents did come to his home; not one but both of them. Sam nodded his head knowingly as they walked through the door.

"In numbers, there is strength, Channa," he said as he asked them to sit.

"I know why you are here."

"Pappa, how could you let him go to a country where there is going to be fighting and killing and war?"

"Can I get either of you anything?"

"Get my son back, Sam. Nothing else," Richard's father said, his voice already assuming the sharpened edge of an ultimatum.

Sam looked at the man seated before him. It was an up and down kind of stare, similar to a sovereign looking upon one of his lesser subjects; a withering look that conveyed his innermost thoughts: "How dare you!"

"I know you are both quite upset," Sam said, softly

enough so that his visitors had to lean closer to him to hear his words. He found a whisper was a much more useful tool than a shout was and in this case he was very right. He waited a moment before he continued hoping quietly that the softening of his voice would have a tranquil effect on them.

"Please remember this is my home and you are always welcome here. This is still my home. I will not fight with either of you. Your son made a decision. I had nothing to do with that decision. Remember it was 'his decision'. He would have gone no matter what I said to him. I only made the connection to what he wanted to do a little, a very little, easier for him. There is nothing for us to shout at each other about, only to wait for his safe return."

Sam did not know exactly how long their words rained down upon him. Their worry seemed to have forced them to speak only of his part in a misadventure they were both positive would end in their son's injury or worse. He knew before it started and after it ended that nothing but dreadfully hurt feelings would come of this visit. When they left he could not be certain that he would ever see or hear from his daughter *Channa* again.

During the weeks that followed, Sam heard from Jacob Ben-Menachem only two times.

"All is well, Sam," was all he would say, despite being deluged with questions from his anxious friend.

"Sam, you promised. Keep your word as I have to keep mine. Shalom."

There was little choice left for Sam but to follow the events in Palestine as they were reported in the Daily Forward. That provided him with the most complete account of the happenings he cared about. He read about the British proposal for the partition of Palestine which the Jews readily accepted. Arabs rejected it wholeheartedly. In addition to their rejection, the Arabs threatened to use force to resist any partition and actually began executing minor raids on some of the older Jewish kibbutzim in Palestine.

The death of President Franklin Roosevelt had a deep and permanent effect on Sam Brandeis. He was one of those that had the wild impression that nothing terrible could change radically for the Jewish people as long as Roosevelt remained the head of the Government of the United States. The impact of his death had Sam shaking his head, unable to make the President's death a permanent part of his being for many, many weeks. He searched long and hard in the Daily Forward to find a discernible change in the US policy toward Palestine but could find nothing of substance.

His phone rang and his friend Jacob Ben-Menachem's voice was in his ear.

"Sam, I know you read about the Arab refusal to accept the British proposal for partition."

"Of course, Jacob, I read."

"This is the best thing that could have happened, Sam because it was turned over to the UN and that is where the final decision must and will come from. That is the place where we will succeed. I have no other news. Shalom."

His voice was gone before Sam could ask any other question of his friend.

Sam followed the paper and he learned of the various attempts by the Haganah to sabotage British vessels that operated in the waters outside of Tel Aviv and Haifa. It was the British mission to catch and deport illegal immigrants trying to make their way into Palestine from boats that were anchored in the harbors around Israel. The Forward printed the activities of many groups operating within Israel that tried to get the British to leave. The blowing up of the King David Hotel in Jerusalem, the military headquarters of the British was one of the Haganah's more successful missions. At the same time that it crippled the British operations severely in Israel, many innocent people were killed. As he read, Sam continually shook his head from left to right; he deplored killings that caused celebrations in some quarters. Attacks on the rail lines were also reported and the liberation of Jewish prisoners from the Acre prison was another success for the Haganah. In Sam's view all the victories on either side were too small to cause happiness anywhere; he felt that diplomacy was the only answer that would bring the homeland to the Jewish people and allow an Arab settlement that would bring some sort of satisfaction for the Arab people as well.

More acts of sabotage were constantly reported on all sides. One action invariably led to another that distanced any peace settlement from reality. Sam digested every bit of news that contained anything about Israel. The possibility that his grandson might be a part of one of them and be in more danger as time progressed clouded his thoughts. He did not enjoy any successes of the Haganah and other organizations in Palestine that took any lives. He knew that every success was at the terrible cost of more lives; lives that could very easily be Jewish lives as well as British lives or Arabs lives.

Sam Brandeis started going to the synagogue more than once every day. He said more prayers, even though he knew that praying in the synagogue would not make any difference to his grandson wherever he was or whatever he was engaged in. He found himself humming *"Hatikva"*, the Jewish Anthem, at various times during the day. It seemed to bring him closer to the young man he cared for and worried about so much.

chapter 12

My Story

THE PILOT INCREASED THE PRESSURE on the engine of the plane and it started to move. The engines roared; the plane rolled slowly into position for a takeoff.

"We're first in the line for takeoff," the pilot announced.

"Will the crew please secure the plane for takeoff and be seated," his voice sounded over the intercom.

I sat back in my first class seat; the plane suddenly came alive; the aircraft, powered by the engines sped down the runway. I had never been in first class and I was looking forward to everything I had heard about the differences between them and the economic seats I was more familiar with.

A final thrust propelled the plane forward and the wheels were no longer touching the ground. I felt the commanding force against the back of my seat and we began our ascent into the night sky. I could see the lights of Boston below beginning to fade. The plane flew into a cloud bank and Boston was gone from view. When we emerged from the cloud bank, I could see the blinking lights of a few planes that were descending into Logan Airport. There were a few stars visible in the sky; there was no moon.

I was about to open the book I brought with me when the man in the next seat touched my arm. He leaned toward me.

"Good evening, Richard," he said.

I looked at him; I had never seen him before.

"I thought it was far safer for us to have as little contact with each other as possible before we took off."

He looked across the aisle and nodded his head; the passengers there were busy making themselves comfortable for the long flight to London.

"I hope the scarcity of information that was provided to you was not too upsetting."

I shook my head. I looked at him again. I was certain I had never seen him before. I decided that the less I spoke, the better it would be until I was certain he was part of what I was part of.

He smiled.

"I know you must be wondering at the manner in which this has been conducted. It will all become clearer when we have chatted a while."

I stared at him. I had received my ticket for this

flight in the mail several days ago. It was a week after I returned from the training sessions upstate.

"The note in the envelope said that you were to take this flight to London from Logan Airport in Boston. I will explain everything you have to know at greater length during the flight. The note said you were to destroy the envelope the ticket came in. *Bon Voyage*."

There was nothing more in the envelope.

"I burned it."

"Is everything I said so far correct?"

"Yes sir."

"Good. It may seem too much like we're involved in an unrealistic spy movie, but there is no reason to take any unnecessary chances. I put those instructions in the envelope which is why I am so familiar with them."

He didn't speak for a moment.

"We have reached our normal flying altitude of 28,000 feet," the voice on the speaker system interrupted our conversation.

"It should be a smooth flight. The weather will not interfere with the time we are due to land in London. If there is any turbulence, we'll be able to climb above it. We should be in London at approximately 6:30 AM, their time. Sit back and enjoy the trip. If there is anything you need, please contact one of our attendants. Thank you."

The voice stopped speaking.

The man seated next to me took a large envelope

from the briefcase he had stowed underneath the seat in front of him.

"This envelope has all the additional instructions you will need and it explains the purpose of your trip, what you are supposed to accomplish and every detail you will need to be familiar with when you are finally on your own. You and I will go over as much as we can carefully so that you understand everything before we land. I will give the envelope to you when we touch ground at Heathrow in London so that you may refer to it at any time you might need to.

I nodded in approval.

"My name is Gidon Ascher," he said. "I am one of the people charged with planning the seemingly impossible task and execution of actions that will secure a permanent homeland for the Jewish people."

"Hello, Mr. Ascher."

"Please call me as Gidon. I believe that people who are comfortable with each other on a 'first name' basis have a closer sense of purpose with each other."

"Gidon it will be from now on."

"There seems to be a small drop of hesitation in your voice and in the look on your face, Richard."

"I'm sorry. So much has happened to me in the past few weeks that I have become dizzy with trust and an actual sense of how I am supposed to react to many newcomers in my life."

"There is nothing wrong with caution. How about if I tell you that I know who your rifle instructor was? She has flame red hair, is as tough as nails, and makes most men feel that they want to reach out and touch her."

"That's a good description of her. I can put my antenna to rest."

"Her reputation says that she can shoot out the eye of a sparrow from 100 yards."

"That's one of the rumors I find very hard to believe."

"Myths spring up easily about a woman like that because she isn't in her natural habitat out on a rifle range."

I had a vision of her naked on the blanket with her legs wrapped around me forcing me to keep my prone position.

"She certainly had all the young men going ga-ga over her, myself included. She was a topic of conversation that some never tired of."

"Her name is Yael, Yael Brenner."

"Doesn't seem to be a Jewish name."

"It probably isn't. Last name is real; she probably just took the first name because it sounded pretty to her. Does it matter?"

"Not at all, not at all."

I felt good that I had a name to go with my sexual fantasies.

"Back to the real world, Richard."

"Right you are, Gidon."

"You will wind up on the Mediterranean close to the shore of Israel after a deliberately round-a-bout route. That has been projected for your own safety, in the rare case you might be subjected to questioning by any authority."

"I understand that."

"You are on a journey to various cities doing research on the Jewish population and various synagogues in those cities."

"I see."

"You are travelling as an investigator and writer. Your bona fides have been provided for you. In the envelope you will find an identification card from the Jewish Daily Forward that indicates that you are employed by them and they have authorized your research."

"My grandfather will love that. He reads that paper every day. Certainly now that I am helping Israel and possibly in a dangerous position."

"The actual names of the synagogues in the cities you will be travelling to are listed in the envelope as well. It should come as no surprise to you that your articles have already been written for you and you can show them in any city where you might run into a problem."

"That will make life easier for me."

"True, but you will have to travel with a small

typewriter in your possession. All the articles that have been pre-written for you have been typed on that typewriter so as to avoid any unnecessary problems."

"Someone must have done a lot of careful planning for all this."

"More than one 'someone', you can be certain of that."

A stewardess came by our seats with water and juice and asked if we wanted anything else to drink. I had made up my mind to drink water while I was in the presence of anyone connected with what I had embarked upon.

"You can have anything you want, Richard. Please take advantage of what is placed before you. That is one of the reasons you will fly first class most of the time you are engaged in any particular activity for us. It raises far less suspicion."

I reminded myself I was only twenty years old and any craziness I pursued with my friends had no place on this airplane seated next to Gidon Ascher.

"No thanks, Gidon, water is fine. Perhaps I'll treat myself to a sip of wine with my dinner."

Gidon ordered a scotch and soda for himself, asked me again if I was sure I didn't want anything stronger than water and waited for the stewardess to get on to the next passenger.

Gidon went over all the aspects of the travel

involved in where I was to go and what I was to do. His explanations were clear and to the point. He stopped short of outlining the actual mission itself.

"Everything I have spoken to you about is clearly indicated in the envelope with details as to people you are to meet, where you are to stay and a rough timetable of this entire trip. It is not complicated and you will have no trouble on that score."

"It seems perfectly clear."

"The important point is that you visit synagogues in all the cities you will travel to so that your ultimate mission can be easily understood by anyone who might question it."

The stewardess came by again with Gidon's drink and told us she would be back soon to take our orders for dinner.

Gidon took a drink of his scotch and soda before he continued.

"You will be flying to each destination, Richard, except the last one which you will get to on a tramp steamer sailing out of Parma de Mallorca under the flag of Spain."

"That's something I have never done before."

"All this has been carefully designed to cover up what you actually have to accomplish."

"I realize that."

"The rest of your mission will be explained to you on

the ship itself. I would caution you only to make certain that you are where you are supposed to be exactly when you are supposed to be there. All else will fall into place easily if the timetable remains perfectly intact."

"It will be as perfect from one end to the other as I can make it."

"Good. Provisions have been made covering all the options and variations we could think of. We have absolutely no trouble relying on your judgment if all does not work out as smoothly or as perfectly planned as it was envisioned."

Gidon Ascher finished his drink and ordered another when the stewardess returned to take our orders for dinner. I passed on the wine.

After we finished dinner, Gidon moved as close to me as he could.

"Richard, your job, basically, is to get three members of the Haganah to the United States. By the time you get to the shores of Israel, they will have been chosen and hopefully they will be hidden, awaiting your arrival on the White Marlin, which is the vessel you will travel on from Mallorca to Israel."

He waited for his words to register.

"They are going to live in your neighborhood in Brooklyn and your basic job, besides making sure that they do arrive in Brooklyn safely and in one piece, is to make them as comfortable as can be and to teach them to be born and bred "Brooklynites". I want you to go over everything they will need for that; language and idiomatic expressions especially, habits, baseball teams, football teams, schools, neighborhoods, etc. In essence they should be able to carry on conversations with anyone else from Brooklyn without stress or mistakes. You will have time with them on the ride home on the White Marlin, which will take enough time for you and them to connect on everything that has to be learned."

I listened, still not comprehending the 'what' or the 'why'. I waited for him to clear that up.

"Their mission is to raise money for what is surely on the immediate horizon. They will be put in touch with wealthy Americans, Jews or non-Jews who have dollars and are willing to help. We will arrange appointments with many of those types of people. There are many available and your three men will sell the necessity of backing the new country with as many dollars as is humanly possible. There is no doubt in my mind that, no matter what the UN decision is, there will be a devastating shooting war that will not be over quickly between the Jews and an alliance of those people who would rather see them driven into the sea. The Haganah will need men and ammunition, many, many weapons of a diverse nature in addition to doctors, nurses, medical supplies, food and transportation which all cost plenty of dollars. They will need time to carry out their missions effectively. It is part of a difficult operation, but as necessary as the correct vote in the UN is. This plan, along with many others, has been in the making for quite a while and now it is time to begin to carry your part out. I am sure you can visualize how important your part in this idea and plan really is.

"I want you to be clear on everything you are expected to do. Of course there will be "connections" to guide you along the way."

He looked at me, waiting for what he said to sink into my consciousness.

I was easily able to grasp what he said and how I was to be a vital part of all those plans they were holding in readiness. I knew there would be a place to get any guidance I might need. I was sure I could do what was expected of me.

"I have no questions, right now, Gidon. I have a request."

"Please, make it."

"I brought a special box with me; I take it wherever I go. It has become a habit since my Grandfather gave it to me. I packed it in my luggage. I would like to keep it with me."

"Of course, that should not be a problem. Keep it with you."

He straightened in his seat. He went over a few more items that he felt needed repeating, like denominations of currency. Then he mentioned that if I was awake during the early morning hours, I should try not to miss the sunrise.

"Check your watch and if it's close to 5:30, stay up. You won't be sorry. We will be flying directly into a most glorious sight."

He was quite correct. I had never seen anything like it before. The sun was a ball of fire when I first saw it in the sky over Ireland. It gradually paled as it turned from a fire red ball to a magnetic orange and then to a golden yellow.

During the earlier part of the night when most of the lights in the cabin were out, and Gidon turned away to try to sleep, I thought of Yael Brenner and then what was expected of me and then of Yael Brenner again. Now that she had a name, she became more of a real person to me rather than just an exciting sexual memory. She was a tangible human being that had taken possession of my youthful imagination. I was not yet wise enough or cognizant of understanding or knowing the sheer and lovely power she possessed. The very same woman who now had a name raised me from an unaware youth to the edge of manhood without my realizing the huge change that she had rendered to my entire being. I still did not understand her indicating that she wanted to spoil me for all the other women who would follow her into my life. If wiser years followed, I would understand.

Our flight landed at Heathrow close to schedule; the sun was close to its zenith in the morning sky. Gidon and I parted in the terminal. I hailed a taxi and went to my hotel in London to officially begin the first stop on my journey.

I was able to include a brief tour of London, including two synagogues and a concert at Albert Hall that evening. I only had a problem with 'wrong-way traffic'. That night, before going to sleep, I checked the flight I had to catch to Barcelona, my next stop in the morning. The small typewriter someone provided for me would hardly become a burden. Two mugs of warm beer convinced me I preferred New York to London when it came to serious beer drinking. I did enjoy a good dinner in a fine London restaurant. By the time I had to catch a taxi back to the airport the next day, I still wasn't used to the 'wrong-way traffic'.

If I would have had any choice, I would have preferred Madrid to Barcelona, as long as I had a stop-over in a city in Spain. I would have enjoyed spending time in the Prado Museum. However, I found the Barcelona waterfront very exciting and I went to a synagogue and a magnificent but yet unfinished cathedral during the day.

The flight to Parma de Mallorca from Barcelona was by far the shortest of the flights. I barely got comfortable in my seat, when the pilot told us he was beginning his descent and we should keep our seat belts fastened until we were parked at the airport gate.

This was the last flight that was listed on my itinerary until I was to fly back to the United States. There was no date listed for my return home so I thought there had to be an amount of uncertainty as to exactly how long my assignments would take to complete. I had been asked during my first interview if sea-sickness was one of my problems, so I figured that I would most probably sail from Parma de Mallorca to some place close to the shores of Israel.

My instructions upon landing in Parma de Mallorca were to look for a sign with 'Dodgers' printed upon it. It would be held high by one of my 'connections' at the airport, who would escort me to the hotel I was registered at. I had a small amount of uncertainty during the flight but thinking about Yael Brenner effectively erased those doubts from my mind and were replaced by more visions of the night we had spent on the blanket in upstate New York.

Everything had been so carefully planned and correctly timed that I was sure that whoever met me at the airport in Parma would fill in any the missing details.

As I deplaned and came down the ramp to the terminal, I saw a sign with only 'Dodgers' printed on it. A man with stained "bell-bottomed" pants and a sailor's hat was holding the sign upright. I waved first and then I walked straight toward him.

"I am Richard, or Ricardo, the one you are meeting."

"Si, Si, Senor Ricardo. I was told to print that word, 'Dodgers" on a sign. I like "Ricardo". I will call you Ricardo. It is familiar to me."

"Almost the same as Richard, but Ricardo is fine."

"Then, *Hola,* I am Capitan Mateo Belmonte, from the ship the White Marlin. *Bienvenido* a Parma de Mallorca, Senor Ricardo."

He actually pronounced my name rolling the second 'r'. I liked the change.

He took my suitcase with the box in it and the small typewriter from me. I did not think I had to mention the box to him. It was in my suitcase, anyway.

"You will follow me, Senor Ricardo'."

"Where are we going, Capitan Mateo?"

"To your hotel in Parma. Tomorrow, very early in the morning, we will go on board the White Marlin. I think there will be some cargo that must be loaded before we leave Mallorca. So, I am not exactly sure when we will leave Parma de Mallorca and sail out to the sea. We will be on the White Marlin tomorrow."

"Then we will spend the whole day tomorrow on the ship? Where will we be sailing to when we sail?"

"Sh, Senor Ricardo. No questions. Later we will talk

about where we are going. I hope you like to sail on ships."

"Will there be anybody else on board, Capitan Belmonte?'

"Right now, there is only you, Senor Ricardo. I was told there might be one more, but no one else has yet come. That is why we will wait until it is dark before we sail. Someone still could be coming. I don't know for sure."

Mateo Belmonte deposited my suitcase, the typewriter and me in a beautiful room with a view of the Mediterranean. He looked around the room carefully. He came close to me.

"We will talk of the destination when we are on the Marlin tomorrow."

"Fine."

"I will be here when the dawn breaks, Senor Ricardo, exactly at the first light in the sky."

"I will be up El Capitan. Will you have breakfast with me?"

"Si, Senor. I'll see you at the breakfast table, downstairs."

"Good. Gracias, Capitan."

"Hasta Luego, Senor Ricardo. At the first light, manana."

"Adios, El Capitan Mateo Belmonte."

As he kept putting Senor in front of my name, I

decided it was a usual term of respect. I didn't think a bit of my 'movie-learned' Spanish would be out of place with this man. He smiled and closed the door behind him. I heard his laughter through the closed door.

After we ate breakfast, I gave El Capitan the address of the synagogue I had to go to. He looked at me strangely, nodded his head and he directed our taxi driver to stop at that address. I went in and he waited outside for me. I was sure by now that anyone that had followed me must be certain that I was a religious fanatic. That included the Capitan as well.

"You need to talk to your God, Senor Ricardo, and you did. That is good," was all he said when I came out. We had to stop for El Capitan to make certain arrangements to pick up his cargo. It was early afternoon when I saw the White Marlin for the first time.

She rode at anchor in the harbor of Parma de Mallorca. She looked like what I thought a tramp-steamer was supposed to look like. It seemed to me that a decent paint job would make a world of difference. I mentioned that to the El Capitan.

"And make strangers we do not know to pay more attention to her," he said. "Not too good, Senor Ricardo, not too good. She is good as she is now."

We boarded her after a short launch ride out to where she was moored. It was a glorious sun-filled afternoon, the kind that makes you glad that you opened your eyes and you felt perfectly eager to be a part of the rest of the day.

After El Capitan had my belongings stowed in what he assured me was the largest cabin on the ship, I went up on deck and looked at the beautiful harbor.

"I will stay only a short time with you here on deck, Ricardo. There is a lot I must do to make us ready to take on cargo before we sail out to sea."

I noticed he had become less formal with my name. I had no idea why, but I guessed we had crossed some a situation where 'formality' was less in style.

"How many men do you have in the crew?"

"From now on, in front of the crew, please continue to call me "Capitan Belmonte." Sometimes there are ten, maybe twelve crew members. I try to use only men from Mallorca, so I know them well and can trust them and they trust me. Before they arrive, I will explain some things to you. First it is better if you have nothing to do with any of them. Even "gracias" is not necessary.

"This trip, we will sail toward the coast of Palestine at a slow speed. No rushing. There is a very, how do you say, perfect schedule I must keep."

"Perfect is OK, Captain. 'Strict' is another way in English to say the same thing. 'Exact' with no changes."

"Ah, that is better, no changes. I will remember. The American Senor who owns the White Marlin and pays our salaries is, as you say, very strict. He tells me by visits or by radio where I must sail and when I must sail and how soon I must come back to Mallorca. He also supplies the cargo we must carry wherever we sail. All is very careful to be correct.

"You will see much, much more when we arrive in the harbor near to Palestine. There is much British activities going on there. You will see for yourself and understand better the need for '*silencio*'."

Capitan Belmonte told me that sometimes he sailed with a full cargo which might consist of chests of tea, bales of cloth or rarely even barrels of wine. When he was delivering those types of goods, he did not go anywhere near Palestine. That was done so that if he were stopped, he could prove that he was the captain of a true tramp steamer, plying his trade. On those return trips he would carry whatever merchandise was needed in the port he finally put into, and return with whatever there was a demand for in Mallorca or some place on the return route where he could make a reasonable stop, either to deliver his cargo or add cargo to his final port in Mallorca.

While he was speaking to me, men kept coming on board the ship. Some waved at him, others passed us by as if we were part of the scenery and still others, those whom he knew better, greeted him. They each gave me the once over and sometimes they seemed to nod knowingly.

"You and me, solely the Capitan and his guest, we will eat at a separate table and maybe even at another time from the crew. We will see. If any other passengers come aboard, they will eat with us, not the crew."

Capitan Belmonte left me as the sun began to slowly set in the Western sky. I did not see him for about an hour until he came to where I was still basking in the warmth of the sun. He handed me an envelope.

"For you, Senor Ricardo, even if they have your name wrong."

I looked at the envelope; all seven letters of my name in English were there together with my last name as well.

"Ah," he said, "that "Dodgers" was supposed to be a code name, no?"

"Si, si, El Capitan, a code name."

"That is as it should be. We cannot be too careful. Please, not to forget, Capitan Belmonte."

"I won't, Capitan Belmonte."

"Your telegram is a big surprise. I leave you to read it at the end of this beautiful day."

"Yes, Capitan Belmonte."

I opened the envelope. It was from Gidon Ascher.

"I have sworn the Captain Belmonte to secrecy. Please check into the cabin next to yours... Pleasant voyage, my young friend and don't overdue."

I had no idea what the message meant. Was it a code

I had missed? I started toward my cabin, got lost twice and finally found it. I looked at the door to the right; there was none to the left. It seemed exactly as it was before. I knocked.

"Come in, Dayan."

I could have screamed when I heard her voice using the special name she had for me, before I even saw her flame red hair. It couldn't be! But it was! Yael sprang from the bed and held me in her arms, as she closed the door.

"No questions; there are no answers. I've got a job to do. Leave it at that. Gidon had Belmonte secretly put me in this cabin late last night. I'll be with you for a while, at least until we get to where we can see Haifa from the ship."

"Yael, we owe Gidon Asher big time."

It didn't take either one of us long to wish the Mediterranean was at least as wide as the Atlantic or the Pacific in a never-ending expanse of green-water happiness. We could have sailed forever, at that moment. We had been given a chance to learn each other; an opportunity that would not be wasted.

All the crew members and especially Capitan Belmonte knew there were no questions to be asked about the woman aboard. Whatever their imaginations imagined, were singly and collectively answer enough.

The White Marlin quickly became our secluded

and protected heaven. We took our meals with Capitan Belmonte. He was the master of discretion, a romantic Spaniard with the heart and wisdom of a nobleman. There was no talk of war at our table, only the glorious weather, the magnificence of the varied colors of the water beneath the White Marlin, and the faultless blue sky above. His knowledge of the particular preparation of the foods we were served proved him to be as close to a chef as one could get without actually being one. The smallest addition that made any course more delectable was not beyond his knowledge or his taste buds. The wines he had served to us with each course could have been ordered by a sommelier in one of the finest restaurants in Paris or from the vineyards of a master brewer in Bordeaux. We returned his urbane charm with no questions about the silver service we ate with, the magnificent dinnerware we used for our meals or the splendid food and wines we were served. Yael or I could not have pictured or blossomed with each other in a more splendid honeymoon atmosphere if we labored for many fevered months over plans for such an excursion. Of course, it was Yael who explained and pointed out to me the true context and luxury of our lives on the White Marlin, as I was far too young to appreciate many of them.

We spoke to each other of the lives we had lived and the other people that were the dearest part of them. I withheld nothing from her and by the time we were out to sea, she knew everything there was to know about me, including my reason for carrying the special box with me.

Several days were spent loading the White Marlin with a consigned and legal cargo that was to be delivered to the British in Haifa. Everything seemed to work with a perfect symmetry as if this was an expected routine by the tramp steamer and its suppliers. We watched with the anxiety of knowing that we would soon put out to sea for the final stages of our journeys and the separation that we knew was imminent.

When the engines of the White Marlin suddenly and with no warning started and the smoke began pouring out of its smoke stacks, we knew the final leg of our journey together was beginning. The sun was still riding in a cloudless sky and when Yael climbed up from her daily swim in the Mediterranean, we stared at each other for the longest moment in the short history of our world. I wrapped her in a towel and my encircling arms could feel a desperation shaking her body as it was shaking mine.

We said little to each other about our departure from Mallorca; there was really nothing to say. I began to take mental pictures of her as often as I could, stockpiling books of memories of her, each an epitome of Yael that I could call up during the coming days and months when we would be apart. Yael managed to keep up her daily routines; the only change I could detect was I felt a new urgency to our love-making driven by her strength, her drive and her determination.

chapter 13

Segue

THE WORLD SEEMED TO BE moving faster in too many diverse directions for Sam to follow carefully with anything resembling a full understanding. His primary interest in Palestine and his grandson were constantly interrupted by important World-wide events. The deluge of global shattering phenomena continued and drowned his main interests by the speed in which they occurred.

The surrender by Nazi Germany buoyed Sam; it caused his heart to leap with a joy it had not known since he gave his grandson the telephone number that led him to Palestine.

The decision by Harry Truman to end Japan's participation in the war by dropping atomic bombs on two cities made Sam cry out in desperation for the innocent lives that were taken. He envisioned the injured that he had seen during the terrible fire at the

Triangle Shirt Factory years ago once again. In dreams, he walked on Hester Street among the dead bodies of the women who were tangled in wounds that doctors had never witnessed before. He awoke many nights in a cold sweat.

The Nuremberg Tribunal, after resurrecting crimes in blood-curdling detail resulted in the condemnation of Nazi after Nazi; killers' names that were hated monsters became a reality as they are sentenced to death one by one. Sam supported those efforts whole-heartedly.

News of Palestine and the many events still going on in that part of the world were obscured by the rest of the world finally arriving at some sort of peace settlement with the Japanese Emperor and his defeated empire.

As Sam's friend Jacob had announced to him in his last phone call, the UN began consideration of a plan for the partition of Palestine, even in the wake of Arab threats to drive every Jew into the sea. Sam waited and worried and waited some more.

chapter 14

My Story

OUR FIRST VISIONS OF THE soil of Israel were not nearly as happy as those of many of the immigrants that were being held on other ships in the harbor of Haifa. Yael and I could see the distant shores of Israel. We could hear cheers again and again as we held onto each other in the sad knowledge that our time together was ticking quietly away.

The British blockade was still being maintained as securely as ever. We had no news that anything of significance had occurred while we were at sea. Any passengers from other ships in the harbor that had the guts to jump off the ships they arrived in were captured in the water of the Mediterranean quickly and detained by the British.

Yael and I could see the blinking lights of many different cities, some of which Capitan Belmonte was able to name for us. Our geography was far from perfect, but it seemed, as it did to so many other passengers on other ships, a 'forever' away.

Capitan Belmonte's smile remained constant, apparently not at all affected by our distance from the shore.

"Not to be concerned, my friends. We are on schedule, but no questions."

After a few days in the harbor, the White Marlin was cleared to deliver its cargo. A very large British Coast Guard Cutter appeared by its side and several men from the British crew boarded the White Marlin. After they went over the ship from stem to stern, checked Yael's and my passports, they signaled to transfer the cargo from the White Marlin to the British Cutter. When the transfer was finally completed, Capitan Belmonte invited their officers for a glass of Spanish wine in his cabin. They politely refused and left the White Marlin.

"Do not worry", he said to us at breakfast the next morning. "The moon will not shine so brightly within a very few days. The night will become darker. We will make our move soon. Be ready. No questions."

Good and terrifying news delivered in the same breath.

That night, clouds covered the sky and most of the moon. A launch was lowered from the port side of the White Marlin which was the side away from the shore and could not be seen unless you were looking for it. It was piloted by our Capitan and he rowed silently into the Mediterranean.

Capitan Belmonte returned in about an hour and summoned us to his cabin.

"Sit, both of you."

We did, looking toward him with great trepidation and some apprehension.

"First I rowed away from the Marlin and then turned toward shore. Then I turned on the engines of the launch and headed toward the land. It was a tomb, very quiet except for the water on the sides of the launch. There is a cove that the launch can maneuver in until it is very close to the shore. The next three nights there will be clouds in the sky over Haifa and they will cover the moon sufficiently. Tomorrow night we will take you there; you will jump into the water miss and swim by the side of the launch till it can go no further. You will then wade to the shore. I hope those you are supposed to meet will be there. I have no answers for questions, so don't ask any. Try to get at least a little sleep. I will check the launch to make sure it is ready to go."

I told Capitan Belmonte that I carried a box with me and I wanted to take it with me when I went with Yael to the shores of Palestine.

"That is not in the plan. What's in it?"

"It is empty now. Gidon Ascher knows about my craziness with the box."

"If Mr. Gidon says okay, it's okay. Does he know you're crazy?"

"By now, I think so."

"Take the box, Senor Ricardo. As to wading ashore with this lovely lady, we will have to see how everything works out tomorrow night. Remember, no questions."

"No questions."

"We knew this was the way we would part, Dayan. We will do what we have to, what we promised we would do."

"Of course, Yael, no questions, but I know we will walk on the soil of Israel together and then I will return to the launch."

"Bring the box, Dayan. You can fill it with some of the sand of Israel and present it to your grandfather. He will love that; I know from what you have told me of him."

"You heard Capitan Belmonte agree. That is my plan."

Yael carried her rifle up on deck; I carried the box.

"What is the box for?" the Capitan asked.

"Sand from Palestine. I will not step on Israeli soil again on this trip. I must get the sand tonight with Yael. Please, Capitan Belmonte, no questions."

"You are crazier than most Americanos I have met and they are all crazy. But, if we can, we will. Otherwise, no questions."

It was a very dark night when we jumped into the Mediterranean from the launch. We floated together holding its side as it inched to the shore.

Capitan Belmonte took the oars and started rowing. The oars made absolutely no sound. The launch moved with his strokes. He turned in sharply toward the shore. He seemed to be listening for any sound. There was none.

Yael and I never let go of each other or the side of the launch. Mateo turned on the motors and sat without moving once again. The only sound I could hear was my heart pumping inside me. Yael took my hand and put it to her breast. I felt her heart beating under my hand. The launch headed closer toward the shore and the Capitan stopped the motors and let the launch drift in toward the shore.

"This is as close as we can get. Get ready to wade. Keep wading as quickly and as quietly as you can. Miss, you go first, in case we must leave quickly."

Yael kissed my hand and waded toward the shore, holding her rifle above her head.

"Now you, crazy Ricardo', you with your box."

I could barely see Yael ahead of me. I followed her shape in the darkness. I watched her walk out of the water. In a moment, I was beside her. When we were both on Israeli soil, she turned to me. She put her free arm around me.

""I love you. Remember me, Dayan, and we will meet in Jerusalem when this is over. Remember, Dayan, my love, next year in Jerusalem. I will wait there for you, forever. I love you."

I was unable to speak. I felt her arm leave me and then she was gone into the soft sand and the blackness. I saw several figures stop her and then they were walking with her. I knew she was safely at her destination.

I kneeled, pressed the lever on the box and put sand into it. I locked it. I straightened up and waded back out to the launch. Several hands took the box from me and pulled me on board. I lay there crying silent tears. I recovered the box when I boarded the White Marlin and went to the cabin and lay down, never so utterly alone.

Describing my true feelings borders on the impossible. The mixture of dread leaving the one I loved was the strongest I could remember after we started back to the White Marlin without her.

"So, my young friend with the box of Palestinian sand," Capitan Belmonte greeted me at the breakfast table the next morning, "you traded your loved one for a box of sand. I thought you were much smarter than that especially with such a lovely woman. I most certainly know it wasn't her idea that she was worth only a box of sand to you."

"The sand is for a man, Capitan, a man you would

admire very much as much as I know you admired Yael. You do a job for what your heart and soul believes in, Capitan, and we do also. I will find her again."

"You know that I was teasing with you, Ricardo. I mean no harm, only a little light talk to ease the pain in your heart. No questions."

"I know, Capitan, but there is no remedy yet for how my heart is feeling."

"Ricardo, tonight it is your turn, but you don't even have to leave the launch. I will take out the launch to a different cove, pick up your three guests, or shall I say 'packages', and bring them back with you. If they get sand in their feet, I can help you get their sand into your box when their feet dry. It will still be Palestinian sand."

I smiled.

"Ah ha, you can still smile. That is good. Sit in the sun, and the day will become night soon."

The sun was warm and mental pictures of my time with Yael began to make a wonderful kaleidoscope in my mind. I was able to ease the longing for her with tiny groups of mini-seconds before the emptiness would return to darken and sadden my day in the sun.

Capitan Belmonte's trip to pick up the three members of the Haganah was not as smooth as Yael's trip to the cove was the night before. He told me he arrived at the appointed pick-up spot in plenty of time to retrieve his human cargo, but they were nowhere to be seen. He waited on the shore for ten minutes, as the arrangements called for and then waded back to the launch and returned to the White Marlin.

"We must go back, Senor Ricardo and make another look for them."

"I will go with you, Capitan."

"Good. I may need help. We will leave now."

I climbed onto the launch from the White Marlin and the Captain rowed us out into the Mediterranean.

"The clouds are moving fast, Senor Ricardo. It will soon let the moon out from its hiding place. We must go quickly. I will turn on the launch's motor now."

We reached the cove where the Capitan had been minutes before. He turned the motor off.

"I see no one, Ricardo. They are still not here."

"We passed another cove a moment ago, Capitan. Could it be that they are waiting there?"

"Maybe. They are not here. I will row us over to that cove. We will go ashore there. Maybe we will find them."

As we approached the shore of the second cove, I saw two shadows in the water. I pointed them out to Mateo.

"That must be them, but there are only two men. I will get them both."

I waded into the water. They told me the third

member of their group was still waiting in the first cove. They had left him there in case we returned.

We got on the launch and Mateo turned the launch back toward the other cove. The other man was there, waiting. Then Mateo moved the launch out of the cove and back toward Haifa; the three members of the Haganah and I made certain we were who we were supposed to be. We had each been given passwords for identifying ourselves to each other. Capitan Belmonte said a few savory curses in Spanish and we all laughed, even though we could only surmise what they meant.

"No questions, Ricardo. None. Our business is finished. We can go home tomorrow to Parma de Mallorca."

I breathed easier when we were able to straighten out all the odds and ends between the four of us. We returned to the White Marlin just as the moon was beginning to show itself from beneath the protective cloud covering that had allowed Mateo, Yael, myself and the three Haganah members to complete the first parts of our missions safely.

I spent the majority of my time with the three members of the Haganah on the trip back to Mallorca.

"You will do your studying below deck in private parts of your cabins," Capitan Mateo Belmonte announced to us on our first day out to sea.

"The crew does not have to wonder any more about

what you are doing here or where the pretty lady with the fire in her hair went. They are loyal, but we have come this far safely. No questions. Our record in this business with the British Navy and the Israelis is still perfect and it must stay that way. All studying and learning is done below deck behind closed doors. No questions."

I felt deprived because the weather was absolutely glorious every day on the Mediterranean. Staying below deck in one of our rooms left me several shades of tan lighter than I had counted on for my triumphant return home. Yael and I had spent many hours on deck, talking, her in the shade and me in the sun. I longed to go back up on deck.

It was difficult for me to bid Capitan Mateo Belmonte a farewell. There were no proper or correct words. I can only say that it was my belief that he felt as empty as I did when we said *'Hasta Luego'* to each other.

None of the scheduled flights were on El Al Airlines, another precaution that had been taken by those that had planned the entire episode.

When I added up the sea voyages on the flight from Mallorca to Barcelona, I knew that I would not be able to honestly claim that my tan was "Israeli". It actually was far more 'Spanish' than it was 'Jewish' anyway.

On all the flights we were seated separately so that any learning, studying and teaching was done on a strictly limited basis. The three of them had plenty to study and absorb; basically there was little time wasted. The three Haganah men had passports that required no explanations and they had no problems at any of the airports we used.

We touched down at Idlewild (re-named Kennedy) in a rainstorm. The gray skies were a change from all the sunshine I had during my trip away. I heaved a deep sigh, not of relief, but one that came from a tremendous longing for Yael. I was going back to my so-called normal life without her or anyone else I had spent several weeks in close contact with. On the one hand, I was certain that I had performed what was expected of me quite well and a great deal of satisfactory accomplishment registered within me. The other side of the same coin indicated that part of me was missing, was going to stay missing and a new form of 'me' would have to take its place. I was not satisfied or happy about that.

The three Israeli soldiers were met by pre-fabricated families, making their arrival in the United States as unnoticeable as any normally arriving family could be. I was introduced to each Mother and Father and enough Aunts and Uncles to fill Yankee Stadium. For a short time we were all part of a delicious home-coming celebration. As far as they were concerned, I knew I had more work to do on their becoming seasoned "Brooklynites" and I would be called on to continue with certain parts of their education, which meant plenty of visits to places I would enjoy. It also meant we would all be seeing each other again soon.

I was suddenly standing alone in the terminal surrounded by fast-paced individuals, each in a hurry to get to the places they had to go to. A different kind of loneliness came over me. I had not contacted any relatives so no one in my family knew I was home safely. I thought that the one exception as to my actual whereabouts would be Gidon Ascher and as the thought crossed my mind, he was quite suddenly standing beside me.

"Shalom and well done, my boy. The whole operation was a complete success. Of course the real proof will be in the amounts of money the three men will raise for their country. Did you find it difficult?"

"I'm glad it's over. Mainly stress. Most of the anxiety during the trip came from the uncertainty of all the unknown people and places which, in the end, proved mainly unnecessary."

"Several things, Richard. First, do you have all your baggage, box and typewriter included?"

"Yes, I do, Gidon.

"Secondly, I would like to sit down with you soon and listen to everything you can remember. Unfortunately, I have to be in Washington tomorrow and then the United Nations for the rest of the week. I'll call you when I'll be back in New York with some time to spare, if that's OK with you."

"OK with me."

"Good. I spoke to Jacob Ben-Menachem when your plane landed. He promised he'd called Sam to let him know you're OK."

"My parents?"

"Your job."

A man in a chauffeur's uniform came up to us and took my bags. I had the box under my arm. I wouldn't let go of the box.

"Richard, you have a limo waiting that will take you home. This is your driver. I see you're still holding onto your box."

"My grandfather gave it to me for my Bar Mitzvah. I am going to return it to him when the United Nations grants Israel its statehood. I filled it with sand from Palestine."

"It will be Israel not Palestine, but in any case, it's a wonderful idea. He'll be very pleased."

"I hope so. To Sam Brandeis it was Palestine, it is Palestine now and it will be Palestine forever to him, no matter what the rest of the world calls it."

"I'll be in touch, Richard. And once again, well done. Shalom."

"Shalom, Gidon."

I told the chauffer I had to make a phone call. He

waited while I contacted my parents and then we drove to my home. It was a sweet ride, made more so by the sound of the rain pelting the windows of the limo.

chapter 15

Segue

As the British mandate ran out, a large portion of the Jewish population in the world awaited the anticipated United Nations action on a State of Israel, certain its time had come.

On the fourteenth of May, 1948, the announcement came, signifying an outbreak of unprecedented joyous hilarity in thousands of Jewish communities throughout the world and furious anger and boiling hatred in many, many Arab areas in other parts of the world. As history indicated in many of the years that followed that momentous decision, the desired result that the United Nations had worked for did not come close to any form of a peaceful resolution.

I met with Gidon Ascher two times at the dilapidated hotel on the West side of Manhattan, but not in the room *Chai*. He asked and recorded, with my permission, hundreds of questions, sometimes asking the same ones over and over again to make sure my answers were the same each time. Gidon waited until the end of our second meeting to ask me about some of the people I had met and the personalities I favored.

"Can I safely assume, Richard, that aside from Yael Brenner, Captain Belmonte was a favorite compatriot of yours?"

"Include yourself, please Gidon. Capitan Mateo Belmonte is a very safe assumption as well. Both of you were great company for me, full of surprises, supremely erudite and as capable at your jobs as anyone could be."

"Thank you, Richard. By the way, I have no news of Ms. Brenner. The last I heard was two weeks ago. She's living in a kibbutz and loving Israel."

"That's fine, that's more than *"dayenu"*. Thank you for telling me."

"Mateo is a very special man. No one seems to know much about him or what makes him tick, or why he is on our side, but I'm glad he is with us. I understand he is quite a gourmand as well."

"In my small time on this planet, the very best. To tell the truth, he is the only man, beside yourself, that I was able to spend any amount of time with. No questions."

"Too bad there aren't any more like him. Richard, I think we have covered as much of your trip as we can.

I will let others hear what you have said and if there are any additional questions they have, I will let you know."

"That's fine with me."

"And as for Ms. Yael Brenner, any word that I receive about her, I will communicate to you immediately. I know how special she is to you."

"Thank you, again."

"Richard, there may be times when the men you brought here will need your help with some minor details."

"I know that. Don't hesitate. I'm ready."

"Very good. Shalom, Richard."

"Shalom, Gidon."

chapter 16

Sam's Story

I FOUND A STORE THAT SOLD wrapping paper that was white and blue and had the six-pointed Jewish star on it. I carefully wrapped the box in it and waited for the announcement from the United Nations, so I could give my prized possession to my prized grandfather.

When the proclamation finally came I hurried to my grandparent's home with the wrapped box pressed tightly under my arm. The schnapps bottle was on the table in their kitchen, with several glasses. There were friends in the room who obviously had joined him in celebration of the decision. They had each already had several drinks. The tears in my grandfather's eyes dripped onto his cheeks and into the smile that seemed permanently pasted onto his face.

"Here, *Richela*, a drink for you."

He filled up a glass to the rim and handed it to me. I took it with my free hand. He held up his glass and we drank together. Then he put his arms around me, and I could feel the happiness overtake him with every breath he took.

"You should drink it all."

"Too much for me, Gram'pa, all in one swallow. But, I will finish it."

"I thought you were a man," he said and everyone in the kitchen laughed. "He doesn't do well with our schnapps or horse radish either. In case you didn't know him, this is my grandson, one of the saviors of Palestine," he announced with pride.

There were sounds of approval and then a few pats on my back.

"I didn't do it all by myself, I had a little help."

"Eva, guess who is here," he shouted. "Come see."

My grandmother walked into the kitchen. She looked at me, put her arms around me and gave me a real sloppy kiss as only she could.

"It is good you have come home. Do not listen to my crazy husband again or he will get you killed."

There was genuine laughter in the kitchen. It appeared that every spoken word was meant for laughter. A good, warm atmosphere for anyone's kitchen on this day.

She tried to take the package from under my arm.

"I see you have brought me a very large deck of cards."

"I could have brought you a case of "bromo" but they didn't have any in Israel. No cards either, Gram'ma. I'm sorry, it is not for you."

I handed the blue and white package to my grandfather.

"For him and not me? He has made you as crazy as he is. Remember, I warned you."

More happy laughter and many smiles.

Sam held the package in his hands for a few moments, feeling its shape carefully while turning it over.

"I think I know what is wrapped up in here, but if I am right, it is not for me. I gave it away once."

I knew he knew it was the box.

"Take the paper off, Gram'pa. It is for you and only you."

The room was suddenly very quiet. The men crowded around Sam to see what was in the package.

He took the wrapping off very carefully.

"I would not want to destroy the colors or the star of our new state," he said.

When he removed the paper, he folded it evenly and handed it to his wife.

"You take good care of it, Eva."

She nodded.

"This box was for your Bar Mitzvah, not to be returned to me. It is yours."

"Open it, Gram'pa."

He pressed the lever and the top sprang open.

"Gram'pa, the sand in the box is sand from Palestine. I put it in there one very dark night on the shores of Haifa. It is for you."

Everyone in the kitchen crowded in more closely around Sam to see the sand in the box.

"That I should live to see this day and touch this sand with my own hand. This sand, that Luca Steiner and his wife Rachel wanted to see and walk on as much as you and I did, Eva. Look, Eva, he brought it all the way from Palestine. It is the sand of the holy land."

I could see he was close to being totally overcome with naked emotion because of the sand in the box and where it came from. He held it close to his chest. I could see he was aching to touch it.

"It's okay for you to touch it Gram'pa. It will not disappear."

He put a finger into the sand and then took a small, very small, handful of the sand and let it run through his fingers. Tears were streaming down his face. He wiped his nose and then his face with one of the napkins on the table.

"Here, Eva, it is for you, too."

My grandmother put a finger delicately into the sand. When she pulled her hand out of the box, some of the sand stuck to her finger. She carefully rubbed two fingers together to make sure the sand she touched ran back into the box.

"Can you imagine how many people would still be alive today if the rest of the sand in that country had been there for the Jewish people fifty years ago?"

"At least Luca Steiner and millions like him," my grandfather said.

"A marvelous gift", a chorus agreed, still pressed around Sam.

I could see that he knew they all wanted to touch the sand, but I also saw reluctance register on his face. I could see him thinking, his head nodding this way and then that way as he usually did before he made a decision.

"Just a pinky, one pinky for everyone and if any sticks, put it back in the box."

He stood guard over the box as each man in the room touched the sand and he made sure every grain was replaced in the box. They all thanked Sam for allowing them their 'touch' and then thanked me for bringing it back.

When each man had had his turn, Sam snapped the top closed.

"It is like drinking the last drop of water in the desert," someone said.

"Sam, you could sell a pinky-dip for a five dollar

donation to the synagogue. Like the ten plagues on Passover," Leon Greene said seriously.

"'*Dayanu*'- enough. No money for this. There can be no price put on it; it is too precious."

Before they left, one of the men said, "Next year in Jerusalem."

My heart skipped a beat as I heard in my mind Yael express the exact same sentiment. The box filled with sand from Palestine turned out to be the finest present I could have given Sam Brandeis.

"I gave the box to you for your Bar Mitzvah. I meant it for you to keep; it is really yours," he said, when all the others had left.

"Gram'pa, you gave me an empty box, one that did not have to have anything in it to have a deep meaning for you. I have filled it with sand that has an even deeper meaning for you. The box filled with sand from Palestine is where it belongs; with you, only you, Gram'pa."

chapter 17

My Story

DURING THE NEXT SEVERAL WEEKS, I was called upon to give very little additional help to the men from the Haganah I had brought to the United States. They had all mastered their tasks and the neighborhoods they lived in. They posed no problem for any official part of the government and they continued to raise money for what they believed in. I was pleased that I had given the time to something positive that I believed in. When I read anything about Israel, I had a warm feeling that I was sure I wouldn't have had if I hadn't been even a tiny part of the founding of the new country.

I had not made any decisions that would alter my way of life. I had no thoughts of changing my citizenship or even going to Israel to live on anything resembling a permanent basis. A visit was always possible but nothing had really changed for me except that the feelings of waste had left me completely.

I began to give serious thought to my future when Gidon Ascher called.

"Richard, can you come to the hotel tomorrow, say sometime before ten in the morning."

"Of course. Is anything wrong?"

"No. I wish to talk to you. A few questions."

I thought I detected a strange sound in his voice.

"I'll be there."

I knew from past experience there was no sense trying to pump information from Gidon Ascher, especially on the telephone. I would find out in the morning.

He hadn't specified a time other than before ten in the morning. I arrived at the hotel at 9:30 and was shown upstairs to room *Chai*.

Gidon was seated behind the desk I remembered from the first time I was in that room. A feeling of trepidation began to come over me; a terrible feeling of the imminence of bad news seemed to be in the air.

Gidon stood up as I entered the room, shook my hand and led me to a seat in front of the desk. He sat down behind it again.

"Richard," he began slowly.

The sound of his voice, so distant and measured, far from the one I was used to confirmed my original trepidations.

"Is she alright?" I asked.

His face seemed to drop; his mouth curled downward.

"Yael Brenner is dead, Richard."

Gidon reached into his pocket and drew out a telegram. He handed it to me. I couldn't see the words and I asked him to read it to me. It was sent to him, asking him to notify anyone he knew that would be affected by the terrible news of Yael Brenner's death. It went on to say that she was a true heroine who had performed her duty exceptionally well. A bomb from somewhere in Syria or the Golan Heights had exploded in the kibbutz where she lived; she and three others were killed.

Gidon was by my side as I began to sob. I felt one hand on my shoulder, the other firmly pressing my arm. I couldn't speak. He held onto me until my body stopped shaking. He sat down behind the desk again.

"I have no words, Richard. I can only tell you that her mission was to train women to work with the Haganah. It was reported to me that she was a great success. It was only a miracle that the bomb found her and went off so close to where she was."

An awful kaleidoscope of memory started inside my head cruelly injecting pictures of Yael lying on the ground into my brain. I felt myself slip off the chair.

I woke up staring into the eyes of Jacob

Ben-Menachem. His lips were moving, but no sound came from them; he was praying.

I could find no peace or solace for what seemed like weeks on end. Nothing made any sense to me. I couldn't talk to anyone; I didn't want to see anyone.

My grandfather called me every day, trying to ease my pain. He couldn't; no one could. He brought Jacob Ben-Menachem and Gidon Ascher to my home one day. Between the three of them, it seemed to get worse until they decided they weren't doing me any good or bringing me any relief from the strangling sadness that gripped my heart and my soul. They left.

I remained in the same state for a little more than another month. Then, I woke up one day not being able to understand why I was allowing my life to remain in a dead state. I reminded myself of my father's Studebaker and wished I had a part that Sam Brandeis could wipe clean and put into working order again into my motor with a few new screws. Then I realized it was me who had to find the part or parts missing and put them in working order again so I could stay alive. The realization that many years were in front of me and were under my control brought me partially back from the abyss. I had to do the rest for myself. I worked out a modest plan.

"I'm going to Israel," I announced the next day at the breakfast table. My parents, who had been told that

I would snap out of the doldrums in my own good time, were astounded.

"Haven't you had enough of that country?"

"It's not the country, Mom. It's Yael Brenner that I must connect with again. We promised each other 'next year in Jerusalem'. I'm not sure of the exact date, but that is not important. I must keep my part of the bargain; she would have kept hers if only she could have. I will be in Jerusalem as we promised each other. Gidon Ascher, that man you met who visited me, will help me."

"You don't think she'll be there, do you?"

"Of course not; she's dead. I know that. I need to make my peace with her and Israel. That doesn't mean I can't keep my part of the bargain, does it? I'm going to Israel as soon as I can arrange it. I will call Gidon Ascher today.

Being in Israel for a week secured my knowledge that what I did and what Yael had done was not wasted. The contrast in the way of life of the people was visible in every way. I could see there was a new aura of the future in the streets, in the stores, on the buses, in the synagogues and in the language spoken. The newspapers were filled with hope even though they warned of a continued basic insecurity until there was a negotiated peace, not only a declaration from the United Nations, holding them together.

I spent several days at the wall in Jerusalem, not

looking for Yael, of course, but enjoying the hustle and the excitement it generated. It was truly 'old' but, in another sense, it was 'new'; a beacon that signified a continuity that had been planted for a people that had finally 'come home'.

The only sightseeing I did was to drive up to Mount Tabor where a stone had been placed for Yael. Gidon Ascher assigned a driver and a small car to me to take me to where it was. It was in a small grove of orange trees that was encircled by a wire fence. It only had her name on it, nothing else.

There was a quiet beauty in the grove that I knew Yael would have loved; she probably did, if she ever visited there. I was happy that I could think of her in that grove and not a human body having been blown to bits. The picture in my kaleidoscope of Yael Brenner and the grove of trees near the top of Mount Tabor became more and more of a comfort to me as time passed and some other precious memories faded.

I decided that while I was in that part of the world, I would stop off in Mallorca before I went home. I thought of Capitan Mateo Belmonte many times when I was paralyzed by the cruel inertia that had me in its grasp due to Yael's death. I wanted to see him again, perhaps even go on board the White Marlin, if it was at anchor in the harbor. I landed in Mallorca with a heightened sense of excitement, anxiety and eagerness at the thought of seeing Capitan Mateo Belmonte and the White Marlin once again.

After checking in at the same hotel I stayed at on my first visit, I made my way to the waterfront. The White Marlin was riding at anchor in the harbor of Mallorca de Parma. I had no way of knowing whether Capitan Belmonte was on board or even in Mallorca.

There was a large brick building near the shore that had an official look about it. A steady stream of men in a variety of sailor's outfits went in and out of the building. I decided they were looking for jobs on the various ships at anchor in the harbor. I thought that if Capitan Belmonte was on the White Marlin, someone in that building would surely know. If he wasn't, they could probably tell me where I might find him.

My Spanish had not improved one bit since the last time I was in this harbor, but I was able to find several men who knew El Capitan Belmonte, understood that I wished to see him and directed me to a bar that was two blocks away.

The *"La Taberna Marineros Viejos"* (the Old Sailors Tavern) had the look, the sound, and when I opened the door, I found it had the aroma as well, of any waterfront bar in almost any part of the world. It was crowded with men; the only women in the bar were waitresses. Every table seemed to be filled with shouting, drinking laughing men.

El Capitan Mateo Belmonte saw me before I was able to find him in the smoke-filled tavern. I felt his arms around me. I was being kissed on both cheeks before I even saw his face.

"Senor Ricardo, you have come back home to your Mallorca."

He held me at arm's length looking me over until we were pushed aside by a waitress with two pitchers of beer, one in each hand.

"Tener cuidado, ojo!" (look out) she shouted at us.

"Come Ricardo to a room where we can be almost alone."

He took my arm and led me to a worn velvet curtain, which he pushed aside. When we were both beyond the curtain, he closed it. There were three chairs set around a heavy, oaken table. The walls were filled with pictures of many sea-going vessels.

"Sit my friend, sit. I will order. It is so good to see you."

He hugged me once again before he sat down at the oaken table.

"What are you drinking these days, my friend?"

I knew his air of gaiety was primarily false, possibly being driven by his need to acknowledge Yael's tragic death. I decided I needed a way to make it easier for him and establish us on a first name basis, as real friends instead of "El Capitan" and his passenger.

"A beer will be perfect, Mateo. I have just come from Israel, Mount Tabor, to be exact, Mateo. There is a small stone there with Yael's name on it. It is set in a small beautiful grove of freshly planted orange trees. I wanted to see it and to say my final 'goodbye'. I kissed the stone and said "Shalom" and then "Hasta la proxima". It was then that I decided to stop off on my way home and see El Capitan once more, so here I am."

"Ricardo, mi amigo, thank you for coming to Parma de Mallorca and including me in your precious trip. We will have a few drinks in her honor and then we will eat in the best restaurant in Parma de Mallorca. After dinner we will take the launch out to the White Marlin. You will stay there tonight in 'your room', which I have never let any other passenger into. It was locked the day I heard about the lady with the flaming red hair. We will talk more and then sleep on the waves. No questions."

We had a few more beers; he introduced me to several male friends who had seen us brush aside the curtain to enter the private room. Mateo made a special production of introducing me to our waitress. She was a black-haired beauty with light olive skin. She bent over to kiss Mateo and held out her hand to me.

I kissed it and she giggled. It was easy to understand why she was so special to Mateo.

"My friend, Ricardo, this is dolce Valentina."

"Hola, Ricardo."

"Buenas tardes, Valentina."

This was greeted by laughter from his friends who were still at our table.

"You are learning, Senor Ricardo. I am hungry. Finish your beer and we will go to dinner. *"Hasta luego, Valentina."*

It was early evening when we had consumed a sumptuous dinner and walked slowly back to the waterfront. Mateo led the way to where the launch was tied up at the dock. When we were in the launch, he drove slowly out to where the White Marlin rode at anchor. Mateo held the launch steady as I climbed the rope ladder up to the deck of the ship. Mateo tied the launch to the side of the ship and followed me aboard.

My head was flooded with memories; I held onto the side of the White Marlin. I saw Yael climbing out of the water and climbing up the rope ladder after swimming in the green-blue water of the Mediterranean.

"I will get some chairs, mi amigo, and we can sit quietly."

I didn't let go of the railing until Mateo appeared with two chairs. He held one of them for me.

"Sometimes, mi amigo, there are memories that can be difficult, especially those that don't want to go away.

"I'm okay, Mateo. I just saw Yael, first in the water and then on the White Marlin. Some memories can be very sad."

We sat together and didn't speak for a while. It grew darker; night descended upon the water and the sky.

"So, Mateo, we did not speak of what you are doing now-a-days. Que pasa?"

"I am still in the freight business. I don't haul human beings anymore, but the freight business keeps me busy enough. I have no complaints. I can work when I want to without any 'strict' schedules."

Mateo had put emphasis on the word 'strict' to remind me of when I told him the correct use of that word.

We both smiled at the memory.

"And your box of sand, Ricardo, did it finally get to its destination?"

"Yes, it did. I gave it to my grandfather on the day the United Nations made the momentous announcement. He was so pleased when I gave it to him and told him where it was from, he cried very happy tears."

"You did a good deed."

"I think so."

"Look at the sky. There must be a million stars up there."

"Yael said that all the stars in the world gathered every night in Mallorca for us. She called it our honeymoon gift."

"She was a very special lady, Ricardo, very, very special."

"I agree, Mateo, very special, much like dolce Valentina."

"I am not too sure about that, but Valentina is wonderful to be with."

Nothing was said for a longer period this time. We both were looking into the heavens, wrapped in our own world of imagination. Mateo broke the silence.

"Ricardo, I have wanted to speak to you of my significant lifetime and when it arrived for me and how it arrived for me."

"Heavy stuff, Mateo."

"What does it mean heavy stuff?"

"*Mucho importante.*"

"Si, Si, most *importante.* I grew up in boats, Ricardo; boats of all kinds. I rowed when I was three; my father had a dory and a row boat. He let me row out to our fishing boat every day, raining or sunshine. When we came back from a day of fishing, it was my job to row back to the shore. I learned to drive a boat with a motor when I was seven years old. My father, he took me out, I don't know, maybe a hundred times until he was satisfied that I could drive the boat with the motor according to the rules of the sea. All the time, it was only boats for me."

"I'm sure that is normal for boys, living so close to water."

"Si, many boys did what I did. It was nothing special,

except I loved it and lived for the boats. It was always a chore for most of the others.

Mateo stopped speaking. He looked up at the sky.

"I wonder if anyone ever tried to count all the stars?"

"I don't know."

"As I grew older," he continued, "I began to want the boats more than the fishing. I became a sailor, like the men you saw at the Taberna. I signed up for many trips. I did whatever I had to so I could get work on the ships. I learned everything there was to learn about sailing a ship and doing all the work that needs to be done on a boat from those trips."

I listened to him as he recounted his early life in Mallorca. I wasn't sure why he was telling me all this, but I was sure there would be a message he considered necessary to articulate to me.

"After many trips and very good reports about me to the owners of ships, I was given my first time as El Capitan. I was proud and determined to be a success because I decided that I wanted to be El Capitan all the time."

"I can understand that, Mateo."

"It was a short trip the first time and the second time. By the third trip I had more trust from the owners. I was very lucky; my two trips as El Capitan were always good. The third trip was bigger in time and miles. I was El Capitan for a ship sailing to Morocco. It was then that I proved that I could be the El Capitan that other men wanted for their ships. I was satisfied with my life."

Mateo became quiet again. I could tell he was coming to whatever the message was that he wanted me to hear.

"The trouble in Palestine caused me to meet a man who wanted me to run the British Blockade with refugees and immigrants, real people. He told me his plan and took me out in the harbor to the White Marlin. As soon as I put my feet on the deck of the Marlin, I felt something very different from all the other ships I had sailed on. I did not know what it was, but I knew it was not the same."

"Is that unusual?"

"I have no way of knowing."

Mateo was silent for a few moments.

"Maybe it was that this ship had a purpose that was more than just hauling merchandise that was only to make money. Maybe it was that the White Marlin sailed for more than just money; it was to sail for a more humane reason. I cannot answer that honestly."

Mateo looked up to the skies as if there was an answer there. I waited for him to continue.

"Sailing the White Marlin the first time was really my "Maiden Voyage", Ricardo. In spite of all the times I had been on the seas, my first sailing on the White Marlin became my Maiden Voyage, the most important one in a life of sailing the seas. I use the words 'Maiden Voyage', because the wonderful man who hired me to be El Capitan of the White Marlin called it a 'Maiden Voyage'. Can you understand that?"

"Yes," I said, "I can understand what he meant and what you felt."

"Good mi amigo. If you really understand, then I can come to the point I was trying to tell you. I think that Yael Brenner was your 'Maiden Voyage', Senor Ricardo. It took me so many years to have it, so many trips sailing on the sea and the ocean that I did not know there was such a thing as a 'Maiden Voyage'. I think it is there for everyone in every life a 'Maiden Voyage' and I think you are lucky because you have already found your 'Maiden Voyage' and you are still so young."

I could only hear the lapping of the water against the sides of the ship when Mateo stopped speaking. I looked up; I found the Milky Way and the Big Dipper in the glorious sky above. Mateo was staring at me, waiting for some kind of a comment from me. I had none.

"There is a time when this 'Maiden Voyage' happened for you", he said. "I think I saw it happen; it must have been with Yael, the woman with the flaming red hair."

I thought over what he said for several moments before I spoke.

"She once said to me that she hoped she had spoiled me for the rest of the women that would come into my life."

"Oh, no Ricardo, I understand what she meant but only for herself; not for you. She was wrong. She didn't spoil you; she made you so much better for every other woman that will come into your life. They will thank her without knowing why or who she was.

"I sailed many voyages, Ricardo, until the White Marlin became my Maiden Voyage. I am not spoiled for the rest of my voyages on any ship. I will always be a much better El Capitan because of the White Marlin.

"Can you understand that you may search for Yael's equal, but that person is not there because you already have had your Maiden Voyage, the perfection you do not have to search for, because you already know what that is. Yes, Ricardo, Yael was your Maiden Voyage. Be ever thankful to her as I am to the White Marlin."

We sat quietly on the ship taking in the most beautiful night; the celestial sky blanketed by shimmering stars without another word being spoken until Mateo asked me if I would like some real Spanish wine. He brought a bottle up from below and we each drank from a bottle of a powerful riojo (red wine).

I found myself eager to continue my own life for the first time in many, many months. I felt a strenuous pull to go below to the cabin Mateo said he kept locked and untouched since Yael and I slept there. I desperately wanted to renew the relationship with my memories of Yael Brenner, sleeping on the sea with her once more, and bringing a complete and total finality to that part of my life. No questions.

I awoke the next morning with a new feeling of resilience; refreshed as though from a long, parched stretch of unnaturally dry emptiness. I dressed and went up on the deck of the White Marlin and felt the gentle ebb and flow of the sea against the sides of the ship. I don't know how long I stood there viewing the sun reflecting off the quiet sea and breathing the clear air of the glorious Mallorca morning.

My sleep had been miraculously and almost totally undisturbed; an occasional interruption of kaleidoscopic memories of Yael, Gidon, Mateo, the waters of Haifa's harbor and the box filled with the sand of Palestine were the only instances I could recall that caused me to twist and turn in my bed.

Quite suddenly, an image of Sam Brandeis was standing on the deck beside me; the wise grandfather who had helped me through the early years of my life with his wisdom and his strengths to this voyage of self-discovery and growth; the fulfillment of the passage that led me from one age to the next. I could hardly contain my eagerness to return home again to share my newest experiences with him and to talk to him once more.